THE BEETHOVEN MEDAL
BY K. M. PEYTON

"There are plenty of nice steady boys you could go out with," her mother told her, but Ruth Hollis knew that beside Patrick other boys would seem insipid and dull. Ruth was quiet, but she had a streak of stubbornness in her nature, and she enjoyed a challenge. When she was younger and crazy about horses, she had always liked to ride the most difficult ponies; so perhaps it wasn't surprising that now, as a girl of sixteen, she should find herself involved with Patrick Pennington—a singularly complex, wild, and talented young man. Nevertheless, Ruth found herself wondering if this particular challenge was going to prove too much for her—with far-reaching consequences for herself and her family.

K. M. Peyton, winner of the Carnegie Medal and the Guardian Award for her distinguished contribution to children's literature, has written a tender, funny, and convincing story of two very appealing young people on the verge of love.

The Beethoven Medal

The Beethoven Medal

K. M. PEYTON

Illustration by the Author

THOMAS Y. CROWELL COMPANY
New York

by the author:

PENNINGTON'S LAST TERM
THE BEETHOVEN MEDAL

First published in the United States of America in 1972.
Originally published in Great Britain under the title
The Beethoven Medal.
Copyright © K. M. Peyton 1971.

L.C. Card 71-175109
ISBN 0-690-12846-0
1   2   3   4   5   6   7   8   9   10

For Mabel George

Chapter One

✸

"Tell me," said Ted, standing at the kitchen window and craning towards the front drive, "am I seeing things, or is Ruth actually mowing the lawn?"

"Oh, hark who's talking!" replied his mother sarcastically. "When did you ever mow it without being asked, might I ask, when you were resident here?"

"Well, I didn't. But then neither does Ruth, as far as I know."

"She does since the baker got a new delivery boy."

"Ho, like that, is it?"

"She mows it regularly at about one o'clock every afternoon, when the bread's due."

"It must be getting pretty bare by now."

"Yes, it is."

"Does he stop and tell her how lovely it looks?"

"As far as I know he doesn't even notice she's there. It's unrequited, this passion of hers."

"What's set her off then? Is he gorgeously handsome? I must have a squint at him. There's a van up the lane now."

"That'll be him. You tell *me* what she sees in him. I'll be interested to know. She has the weirdest taste in boys. Your father and I get worried about her at times. We worried about you once, I suppose. Well, you were bad enough, but a sixteen-year-old girl just about takes the biscuit. She was a lot easier when it was all horses."

Ted, aware that his own disastrous marriage did not prompt his mother to view Ruth's affairs with much opti-

1

mism, did not pursue the subject, but he was curious. Six years older than his sister, he had always thought of her as a scruffy kid and, looking at her thoughtfully through the window, he could see little to make him change his mind. She wore jeans with holes in the knees and a faded blouse: she was slight and thin, with no figure to speak of, all wire and sinews to Ted's way of thinking, due to too much hard riding of fast ponies. She was quiet, not a party type like his Barbara—which might even be an advantage, he thought with a slight bitterness. Who was to know what anybody saw in anybody else anyway, save themselves? What was the good his mother asking? It was just chemicals in the blood or something. He wished often that his chemicals had never got involved with Barbara, but an innate optimism kept him buoyant through the domestic trials of his own home life. All the same, he was interested in Ruth's baker.

"If you want to study him, you can tell him a large uncut," his mother said. "Give him a shout—he usually leaves it in the box by the gate, but I want to pay him today. These boys—they're always in too much of a hurry to stop for the money. They run you up a bill as long as your arm —they drive you mad."

Ted thought privately that it wasn't a job he would go much on, trying to please a load of fussy women. He saw the van crashing through the pot-holes towards their front gate, and went out into the garden, smiling at Ruth's tense nonchalance at the lawn-mower.

"Ma says a large loaf, uncut, and tell him to call for his money," he told her.

"You tell him," she said, with a quick, scared desperation.

He laughed. The color flared up in her cheeks. Ted, remembering what it felt like, turned away and went back into the kitchen.

"I put the money on the mantelpiece," his mother said,

smoothing a sheet over her ironing-board. "It's right. You give it to him."

"She's got it badly," Ted said.

"Hmm!" It was more a snort than anything else. The iron went down with a bang. "That sort! You've only got to look at him——"

Ted looked at him, tolerant towards his sister's fancy. He saw immediately that the boy was not the sort to please mothers, being offhand and long-haired and as scruffy as Ruth herself. He was tall and powerfully built, but moved with an aggressive ease; there was a scornful, belligerent air about him that suggested to Ted that he could easily get into trouble, although Ted suspected that not many would want to tangle with him. Ted recognized instantly what it was that attracted Ruth, and no doubt many other girls as well, but to his mother—too far gone—the boy was merely truculent and without charm. He did not smile, or say anything at all, ticking off the payment in the book, handing in the loaf, and retreating with the basket slung over his arm, hands in pockets, shoulders hunched.

"Loads of sex appeal," Ted said to his mother, grinning.

She brought down the iron with a crash. "You two!" she said. "I don't know what I did to deserve it!"

"Poor Ruth," Ted said, with genuine sympathy, remembering.

"Poor Ruth be bothered! Mooning about all day like a lost thing. Now she has no exams she seems to have no aim in life at all, a face as long as a fiddle—she makes the whole house miserable. She never goes out, yet there's lots of boys round here call for her, all decent, respectable boys most girls would be only too happy to go out with. That Gordon Hargreaves—he's even got his own car since he passed the test, and he's always asking after her, a really nice, well-mannered lad——"

3

Ted let out a terrible groan, and his mother's face closed up, anger whisking in her eyes. Ted got up to go, knowing that the abyss had opened; they were on different sides, irrevocable. Poor Ruth! Decent, wet Gordon Hargreaves . . . ! Did his mother not remember, even a little bit, what it felt like? Was she honestly blind, at forty, to what made the baker's boy different from good Gordon Hargreaves with his polite muff's face? Ruth, who had always taken everything so hard, starting with her first pony—quiet, vulnerable Ruth—had an implacable will, and would do, Ted knew, exactly what her stubborn inner voice directed, and would not love her mother's choice.

"I must get back to work," he said. "Thanks for the dinner."

"You're welcome."

His mother gave a short sigh.

He walked down the long rutted path to the gate. The lawnmower stood abandoned, and Ted was surprised to see that the van was still at the bottom of the drive, obstructing his exit on the motor bike, and that Ruth was talking to the baker's boy. Aware that she would never have got into conversation with him on her own initiative, he was immediately curious, and went up to them with his usual candor.

"What's up?"

The boy turned around and said with a vehemence that surprised Ted, "I've cut my finger on the ruddy door." He spoke as if it were a disaster of the first order, yet to Ted it was merely a scratch, bloody but insignificant.

"Mother's pride, with spots on," he said, looking at the loaf in the basket.

The boy said something very rude about the bread, and flung the basket in the van.

"Go up to the kitchen and run it under the tap," Ted said.

"There's some elastoplast in the cupboard. Ask Mum."

"Yes," said Ruth, all shining at the opportunity. "You can't leave it like that, because of the bread."

They all walked back up the path, Ted grinning at Ruth's luck. He couldn't get out until the van was moved, and he liked interesting situations.

"Now what?" said Mrs. Hollis, still sour from her thoughts over the ironing-board.

"A mortal wound," Ted said. "Blood-enriched bread . . . extra nourishment——"

"Oh, shut up!" Ruth said angrily.

"Put it under the tap," said Mrs. Hollis. "There's some sticking-plaster somewhere."

She went rooting in the pantry. The boy ran the finger under the tap and studied the ragged little wound with an intent scowl. His hands were large and the fingers, flexible, square-tipped, gave an impression of uncommon strength. Good strangling hands, Ted thought, having watched a pair doing their work on the television two nights previously.

"Oh, cripes," said the boy. "What a flaming——" He cut off the next word in time, catching Mrs. Hollis's eye, and shrugged.

She held out a plaster strip.

"Haven't you got any disinfectant?" he asked.

The Hollis family, who by nature were not fussy about their health, all eyed him with suspicion, even Ruth. Ted sensed her disappointment, and smiled. Mrs. Hollis produced a bottle of Dettol which had been mostly used up, Ted remembered, on the cat's leg when it got bitten by a rat, and the boy bathed the finger with immense care. They all watched in silence. When it was dry again he put the dressing on, fixing it with a gravity out of all proportion to what was involved.

"I hope it won't be too painful," Mrs. Hollis said.

5

Made aware by her voice of the lingering scorn in the atmosphere, he looked at her angrily, opening his mouth to say something. But whatever it was to be, he thought better of it, for he turned away very abruptly, and went out of the door without a word.

"Thank *you*," said Mrs. Hollis scathingly, when he had gone. She picked up the iron again. "Get along with you, Ted. You'll be late."

Ted went down the garden path again, and Ruth came with him, silent. They watched the van leap off down the lane, and Ted took his crash-helmet off the seat of his motor bike and put it on.

"He's a raving hypochondriac, Ruthie," he said.

"Oh, he isn't!" she flared back. "He——" But she had no defence to offer, and shrugged. "He's a student," she said. "His name's Pat."

"How do you know? You never asked him!"

"The other baker told me."

"Student of what? Medicine?"

"Oh, shut up!"

"Pat . . . Patricia," Ted grinned, kicking his motor bike into a strident roar.

"I hate you!" Ruth screamed at him through the din. "You're beastly!"

She was so easy to tease, Ted could never resist it. He laughed, ignoring the hint of shame put up by his better nature, let out the clutch and roared away down the lane. He had bigger problems than Ruth, but if he told her that she would never believe him.

Ruth flung herself down on the grass, not wanting to hear any of the remarks her mother was bound to make if she went back into the house. She felt cruelly cheated by the way things had turned out. The incident, full of the most lovely promise, had been turned to sour disappointment. Ted and her mother had ruined it. She could not bring herself to admit that this marvellous boy was himself the cause of her disappointment. Ruth's heroes weren't sissies; their physical courage was boundless; they were reckless and debonair and cared for no man. Pat, until today, had been full of promise; she had loved him desperately. But now . . .

Ruth plucked at a blade of the overcropped grass. She had broken her collar-bone once, in a riding fall, and finished the day out. One just did, according to her code (of course, she hadn't known it was broken until later). Her father was always laughing at her. He called her an incurable romantic, but she didn't see why. "Come down to earth," he said. But at least he laughed; he didn't get exasperated like her mother. Ruth groaned. Everything she did lately seemed to annoy her mother, but Ruth would not admit that any of it was her own fault. Vulnerable over Pat, Ruth would not approach her mother now; she lay flat on the grass, feeling the warm sunshine through her blouse, liking the quiet.

It was quiet where they lived, out of the village, away from the new housing development, in an old cottage which her father had done up, using his own skill and ingenuity rather than money. Ruth had always loved it. In fact, she still loved it, but lately everything had got all tangled up in what she liked and what she didn't like, and sometimes she wished she lived on her own somewhere, where she could do as she pleased. She wasn't due to leave school for another year. She was nearly seventeen, and she didn't really know yet what she wanted to do. Her mother wanted her to do typing and book-keeping. "Something useful," she kept saying. The only thing Ruth wanted to do was to work in a stable like her friend, but there was great opposition to this plan both at school and at home. "Unworthy of her intelligence," they said. As if intelligence was completely unnecessary when it came to running a stable of valuable horses . . . Ruth, hating them all, had lately decided that, if they wanted her to be an intellectual, she would stick out for art school. There had already been some preliminary skirmishes on this idea.

"But what good is it?" her mother had asked, appalled.

Ruth sometimes thought her mother never *saw* anything —only the holes in one's tights, and fluff under the bed. The night before they had been to see a film in Northend. To Ruth it was a beautiful film, touching and sensitive and visually breathtaking, and she had come out into the street in a state of ecstatic bliss.

"Oh, it was lovely! Lovely!"

And her mother had said, very sharp, "It was disgusting! Disgusting!"

"Disgusting?" Ruth had recoiled, as if her mother had struck her. She had had to adjust, to try and see what her mother had seen, and the shock of it was like a pain.

"It's you——" she started, almost crying. "It's——"

"Fish and chips everyone?" her father had put in rapidly. "If we sprint we'll beat the line. Quick, Ruth, you're the fastest!"

And she had run, the street all lights in the warm rain and the smell of the sea coming up with the traffic, and she was choked with such a maze of emotions that they ran into a great choking confusion like the lights in the wet road. She had cried, and had no idea what she was crying for, only that she wanted to be on her own somewhere and think her own thoughts and just—just *be*. She kicked at the over-mown grass.

Her mother called out of the kitchen door, "Ruth, are you going into Northend this afternoon? You'll miss the bus if you don't go and get changed now."

"I'm going like this," she called back.

But she got up, brushing the grass off her front, and went slowly to the kitchen.

"You can just pop this suit of your father's into the cleaners," her mother said.

There were only four buses a day out of the village. Ruth combed her hair, looping it back over her ears, which did not hold it for long. Her mother was always saying it was a mess, but Ruth liked hair just as it came, long and straight. She did her eyes, changed into a pair of jeans without holes in it and fetched her library books, stuffing them into the basket with the suit.

"You'll be back on the five-fifteen?" her mother asked.

"Yes. Unless anything wonderful happens."

Once she had missed a stipulated bus because she had been offered a ride on a thoroughbred which had won six point-to-points, and beside such bliss, in those days, the times of buses lost all meaning. Now the phrase was a family habit, to cover such eventualities.

Amazingly, something wonderful happened before Ruth was five minutes away from the house. Walking up the lane, she heard the noise of an engine coming up behind her and moved over to give the vehicle room. As she did so, she knew that the engine was that of the baker's van; she recognized its particular note, having listened for it so avidly during the last couple of weeks. She also knew that the round was finished and the van was going back to Northend, and there was no time at all in which to think or rethink. She turned and put her hand up and the van came to an abrupt halt beside her. The boy looked at her coolly out of the window.

"Can you give me a lift into Northend?"

"If you like," he said, without any joy.

She went around to the other side and he leaned over

9

and opened the door for her. She got in and closed it, and sat looking straight ahead, her heart thudding so loudly that she felt its noise filled the whole van. The air was suffocatingly hot beneath the tin roof in spite of the open windows, and the smell of fresh dough and spiced buns, laced with engine fumes, was thick in Ruth's nose, so that she felt almost faint. She had a quick, pinprick vision of herself falling against the hulking shoulder beside her, and him having to lift her up and carry her out into the shade and kneel beside her, smoothing her brow. This dream she hastily banished, to cool her palpitations. Her mind then went quite blank so that they drove on in silence, the van cavorting through the pot-holes at a pace a good deal too fast for its constitution.

Pat drove with his elbow out of the window, pushing the old van, but his reactions were quick and Ruth was not worried for her life, merely for her complete inadequacy to rise to this fantastic opportunity. Having in that impetuous moment acted out of character, she now found it impossible to follow up the suggested role of the easy, uninhibited hitch-hiker; her mouth was as dry as the last of the buns in the back of the van, her vocal chords fixed in silence, and she was forced to stare straight ahead at the undulating road like an imbecile, her inside tense with an agony she had never experienced before.

Pat was equally silent. Ruth put his silence down to pure boredom, and was mortified further. The van ground over the ridge above the river valley where the village lay, and the dual carriageway opened up before them, sweeping down under the line of pylons towards the arterial beyond. Ruth could see the new high blocks of Northend, and the glimmer of the sea; they were half-way there and neither of them had yet said a word. Pat changed back into top gear and the van sped down the white curving road, the cooling wind streaming into the van. He turned and glanced at her.

"You going shopping or something?"

"Yes."

The word burned her throat. She stared down at the floor. She thought of Ted's easy way, his teasing, and a sharp despair prodded her.

"You—you——" She was like a fish on a quay, gasping and flapping. "You've finished now?"

"I reckon to be off by two, yes."

They had come to the clover-leaf which gave access to the arterial. He put the van into third and roared up the slip road, turning to watch the line of traffic he had to join. A tanker went by, and he slipped in behind it, and almost immediately pulled out to overtake.

"The rest of the day's my own," he said, with a slight bitterness.

"What do you do?" Ruth found she was getting back into the habit.

"Oh, I work," he said.

"What, again?"

"Oh—it's different. I mean study."

"You're a student?"

"Yes."

"What of?"

He didn't say anything, pulling out to overtake again, watching in the mirror. When they were back in the inside lane he said, "Zoology."

Ruth's ideas had to be reshuffled to take this. She had supposed engineering or something mechanical. He wasn't the conventional university type. His manner and attitude suggested a hard upbringing, and there was no suggestion of affluence and very little of refinement in his appearance, which she supposed was why she had imagined a subject severely practical. Zoology, to her mind, was as rarefied as her mother considered art to be. It meant nothing at all to her, except zoos. She could think of nothing to say on the subject at all.

"You still at school?" he asked her.

"Yes, I've got another year. Then I'm going to art school."

He made no comment on this, possibly as thrown by art as she was by zoology. She was easy now, warmed by the fact that he had spoken to her, wishing they were going to the north of Scotland. They were already slowing down for the roundabout and the turning into the town. He was concentrating on watching for an opening, his foot hovering over the accelerator. Ruth looked at his hands on the wheel, the finger with the sticking-plaster on held out, away from contact; his arms were very hard and muscly. She wondered if he did weight-lifting, and hoped not. She could not place him, somehow. He did not fit into any particular pigeon-hole: an uncouth student, a hypochondriac he-man, a zoologist baker's boy: it was all contradictions. It did nothing to damp her admiration for him at all. It just added to the fascination. Usually the physically attractive boys were terrible let-downs when they opened their mouths and better left unapproached on their pedestals, but this time Ruth knew that she was badly committed, and heading for a painful heartache. It was a very happy thought.

She said, because she wanted him to talk again, "What's your name?"

"Pat."

"Pat what?"

"Pat*rick*."

It was a snub in a way, but offered in a perfectly agreeable tone.

"Are you Irish then?"

12

"My mother's Irish."

They were threading their way rapidly into town. The time was running out.

"Where do you go to university?"

"In London."

"But you live here?"

"Yeah—I come home in the vacations, that's all. Get a job, work—if you can call it a vacation."

"Don't you get a grant?"

"Yes, I've got a grant, but you need more than that, for heaven's sake. Do you want to get out along here somewhere?"

"It doesn't matter where I get out," Ruth said, wanting to go all the way. "I'll get out where you do."

"The bakery's round the back of the Parade. That do?"

"Yes."

He pulled up for the traffic-lights, and sat drumming his fingers on the wheel, staring into space. Ruth wanted to ask him where he lived, but did not dare. She wanted to ask him how old he was, how many brothers and sisters he had, what he did in his spare time, whether he had a girl-friend, what his surname was, what he liked to eat, where he liked to go . . . she could feel the minutes running out, and she was struck dumb again. It was impossible to speak.

He made a patient right turn, probing a gap in the oncoming traffic as the lights turned again. The van threaded its way up a congested street and turned into a yard, to meet a brother smell of dough and spiced buns, stronger and fresher than the faded aromas of the van. Pat parked in a row of identical vans, switched off the engine, and sat back.

"That's it then."

It was as good as saying, "Get out." Ruth got out. She

13

stood beside the van, looking at the ground, holding her basket.

"Thank you very much."

"Any time," he said, very casual. He pulled his money-bag and the ledger out of the van, slung the bag on his shoulder, and went away towards the office. He did not look back, or say good-bye, or give even a flip of his hand in salute. Ruth wondered, for a moment, whether it was worse than the whole thing never having happened at all. She felt flattened, humiliated by her own inadequacy to prove any sort of an attraction at all.

She walked slowly out of the yard. The inadequacy—not even to be able to speak, let alone make bright, intelligent remarks—speared her. He must have thought her a complete half-wit. The glib advice of the *Marybelle* comic floated through her brain: "Be *bright*—be *interested!* Ask him about his dreams, his fears! He is just as shy as you at heart!" Ruth doubted it somehow. In *Marybelle* he would have dated her, and they would have had a fab time. But things like that didn't happen to her. She crossed the road without seeing anything, walked on up the road and came to a halt at the traffic-lights they had passed earlier, hardly aware of which direction she had to go in.

"Hi," a voice beside her said.

She nearly jumped out of her skin. It was Pat, on a bicycle, stopped for the red light.

"Don't spend too much," he said.

"Oh!" The *Marybelle* things danced through her brain, even as her mouth gaped open and the color flared up in her cheeks. She stared at him.

"Cheer up!" he said. "You'll soon be dead."

The red light changed to amber.

"Don't do it," he said.

"Do what?"

He put his hand up and made a throat-slitting gesture,

14

gave a passable imitation of a death-rattle, and cycled away through the snarled traffic. Ruth leaned against the traffic-light, utterly vanquished.

"Who told you?"

"Mrs. Pargeter."

Ruth glowered at her mother. "I thought you said that the thing you hated most about villages was village gossip. I thought you didn't take any notice of it."

"No. I'd *rather* not take any notice of it. In fact, I didn't take any notice of it, until Mrs. Brown said she'd seen you in the baker's van, presumably on your way to Northend. That puts a slightly different complexion on it. In any case——" Mrs. Hollis looked up from the potatoes she was peeling and gave Ruth a long, hard look—"I'm not making an issue of it. I'm merely passing on what I was told."

"Gossiping."

"Be careful, Ruth."

Ruth shook her hair back angrily. "Well, what does it matter? People are put on probation for absolutely nothing. Just—just going over the speed limit or something. Did she say what it was for?"

"No. She just said that she had lived next door to the Probation Officer in Northend and knew that that boy— Pat whatever his name is—was one of his—er—clients, I think was the word she used."

"What is it anyway?" Ruth asked crossly. "This probation thing?"

"Well, it's used if someone comes up in court for an offence not bad enough to be sent to prison. They're fined and put on probation, which means they have to report to this Probation Officer at regular intervals, and he keeps an eye on them, sort of thing—tries to stop them getting into any more trouble. Helps them really."

"Well, it's not a bad thing then."

"No, I didn't say it was. I wouldn't have bothered to tell you about it at all if it wasn't that you're so *interested* in the boy. I just thought you ought to know."

"It couldn't be a bad thing else he'd never have got a job with the baker's. Handling money, I mean."

"No."

"She's probably got it all wrong anyway. Gossip's hardly ever right."

"Well, she knew his name and where he lived and everything. I don't think she'd got it wrong."

"What is his name, and where does he live?"

"I'm sure I wasn't interested enough to remember."

"You remembered the other thing!"

"Oh, Ruth, let's not argue! We're coming very close to it . . . lay the table. Let's not talk about it any more."

"You started it——" Ruth bit at the words, too late. She saw her mother's face. "I'm sorry, I'm sorry! It's just that —oh, it's not fair! It's——" She stumbled, close to tears. "Oh, it doesn't matter. I don't care."

"Put the beetroot out, and that jar of pickles."

Sometimes, when her mother was reasonable, it was worse than when she was just plain angry. Ruth crashed everything on to the table. None of the whole silly thing mattered anyway, not even if he was a murderer. He wasn't interested in her, and was probably madly in love with another girl. No doubt there were female zoology students with far more charm than herself, as well as the baker's office girls, and girls at home. She fell into a dream, trying to imagine his home, and him looking at things under a microscope all afternoon and making notes, and studying into the small hours. It was very difficult, with so little to go on, and not knowing where he lived, or what his parents were like, and after a little while her mind went back to the information supplied by Mrs. Pargeter, and she fell into another dream, in which he beat up a party of thugs who were annoying a lovely young girl (herself), unfortunately killing one of them so that he found himself in court on a charge of manslaughter. The judge commended him for his chivalry, but was compelled to find him guilty, and put him on probation for three years. This kept her in a trance-like state all through tea, and her mother said: "The trouble with you is—you haven't got anything to do, since that pony went away."

"When I had him you said I spent too much time with him."

As this was true, Mrs. Hollis made no reply, choosing to ignore the tone of voice in which it was stated. Ruth, still in her dream, wandered down the garden to the empty stable, and leaned over the door, picking at the splinters of wood, sniffing in the nice smell of old hay, of cool shadows and spiders' webs and things past, wishing she was at peace, wondering how it ever happened: the dull imperturbability of being adult. They had no feelings, no bliss, no agony. It was all the same to them; a little worry was very much the same as a little joy. Nothing they felt was the whole world as it was to her. Ruth groaned and hung over the door, her arms dangling. "I love you, oh, I love you, Pat*rick*," she said to the echo of the old loose-box. A few weeks back she could have said it into the mane of dear Toadhill Flax, and received a slobbery nuzzle for comfort, but Toad had cut his leg so badly in a jumping accident that he had nearly had to be put down, and now he was turned out for the rest of the summer up at the McNairs', recuperating. The McNairs had owned Toad in the days of his youth, so he was at home in a sense—Ruth had no doubts for his happiness. Only her own.

"Oh, Pat*rick* . . ." she said, and it meant a thousand thousand things—half things and fragments. She didn't know what. It was all tangled up like the winter fuzz of the wild clematis that had died and still hung in one of the old pear trees; it was as insubstantial as the smell of the absent pony, the fluff of the dandelion clocks that disintegrated around her ankles as she walked through the grass. She put out her arms and shut her eyes and revolved in big circles on the grass.

"I—I——" She didn't know what, she didn't know anything, but felt as if it was all at her finger-tips, and she blundering and sensing into it like the summer moths, knowing nothing, and feeling everything.

"The girl's barmy," her mother said sharply to her father, shaking the table-cloth out of the back door.

"They all go through it," Mr. Hollis replied, reading the evening paper.

"It's me that goes through it," Mrs. Hollis said. "Oh dear, I can see it all coming——" She ran the hot water into the washing-up bowl and gave it a shot of detergent. "It's starting all over again, like we had with Ted."

"Oh, rubbish."

"You see. You just wait."

Chapter Two

✳

Ruth was clipping the hedge, her heart shaking her. The van pulled up with a scrunch on the dirt and he got out and went around to the back of the van. Ruth dropped the shears and went down the path, wondering if her voice was going to work. "I'll take it," she was going to say, very casual. "I'll take it," she practiced, her lips moving. She got to the van and stood staring at him, her lips parted, silent.

"One large uncut," he said, and handed her the loaf. She took it, and one of his fingers brushed hers for a fleeting fraction of a second. She looked at them, withdrawing, and the sticking-plaster, and said:

"How is—you—how——" Oh, God, she wanted to die! She was so hot, she was burning.

"You do anything Sundays?" he said.

"I generally go up McNairs'." Pure astonishment prompted her. She sounded quite normal.

"Oh, it doesn't matter." He slammed the van doors shut.

"What?" She must have misunderstood him. She clutched the loaf, wild with fright at her words. "If—if I've nothing —nothing else—I——" Oh God, again!

"I've got to go to London on Sunday. It's work really, work-cum-pleasure. I thought you could come, but it doesn't matter, if you're doing something else."

"Oh, no!"

"You won't come?" He was getting back into the driving seat. "It doesn't——"

"I will come! I will come!" Ruth said, frantic.

"Okay. I'll be on the one-fifteen from Northend. I'll be at the front, and lean out for you at Wickside. Will that suit you?"

"Yes."

"See you."

The van leapt into gear and disappeared in a big cloud of dust down the lane. Ruth clutched the loaf and walked up the garden, seeing nothing, white as a sheet.

"Oh, good heavens, what's the matter?" her mother asked. "Are you ill?"

Ruth sat down at the kitchen table, and stared at the loaf.

"He's asked me out."

Her mother's reply was one syllable: "Oh." It had more feeling in it than the whole two sentences that had gone before. It jerked Ruth. Cold feelers of apprehension prickled her.

"You can't stop me!"

Her mother gave her a hard look. "I never said anything, did I?"

"You won't? You can't!"

"I can, Ruth. But I won't. As long as I know what the plans are."

"He's taking me to London."

"I beg your pardon?" Her mother looked astounded. "To London!" London from where they lived was a once-a-year place, for the sales, or Christmas, unless you were a long-suffering commuter with an expensive season ticket.

"He said he's got to go up for his work. 'Work-cum-pleasure,' he said, and would I go."

"His work? Delivering bread, you mean? To London?"

"I thought his other work. The student part. The zoology. Perhaps he means the Zoo." Ruth's face cleared. "Yes, of course. The Zoo. It's a Sunday sort of thing, isn't it?" And so eminently respectable, full of parents and children, grandparents even, not layabouts and hippy lovers. Ruth smiled, a wide, sweet smile of utter bliss. "It's all right? It is, isn't it?"

"Yes, it's all right, with reservations. We'll see." Mrs. Hollis sighed, and went to put the kettle on for a coffee. "You choose them, not me." She fetched a bottle of milk, and peeled off the cap. "Just behave yourself, that's all I ask. You know what I mean. He's a bit different from the boys you're used to, more experienced in the ways of the world, from the look of him. So be careful."

Later, when she was alone with her husband and Ruth was in bed, she said, "What else can you say? If you say no, it's immediately turned into a tragedy on the scale of *Romeo and Juliet*. But if she spends a day with him, he can't possibly live up to the image she's made of him. He's bound to be a let-down—so here's hoping."

Her husband laughed. "I take it you don't approve of him?"

"He's a mannerless yob, as far as I can see."

"We'll have to meet him—the bread-round apart. He's probably all right. It's the way these days."

"You're a born optimist."

"Yes. But of course. I'd never have married you otherwise."

You could see the train coming for a long way, as the line was straight for a good mile out of the station. Ruth saw it coming and shut her eyes and prayed to God, "Please let it be all right! Please let it be lovely." She was terrified he might have thought better of the idea, and gone on an earlier train to avoid her. If he wasn't looking out of the window she would have to wait for the next one, or go home. She would die, she thought.

She stood at the top of the platform, and the train grew

big quite suddenly, and there was a head looking out. Seeing him, the relief was like an explosion. Ruth ran, and he pushed the door open.

"Hi."

"Oh, hullo! Hullo."

Ruth felt as if she had been running for half an hour. The carriage was a walk-through one, with quite a lot of people in it. He waited for her to sit down, and sat down opposite her, and looked out of the window. Ruth looked at him, but didn't say anything. She was perfectly happy, it didn't need anything else. And it was so fragile, the start of it, she was so frightened of it being broken that she would dare nothing. But sit.

He was wearing fawn-colored needlecord jeans and a plain brown pullover and scuffed suede shoes; he was neither smart nor scruffy. He had combed his hair, which was brown and slightly curling, long by her mother's standards but not by hers. He was completely non-committal in his assumed appearance, but his native expression still had this quality which Ruth found so compelling. She could not put a name to it, save that it was quite opposite to any expression she had ever found in Gordon Hargreaves' face, even at his most animated. It was nothing to do with being handsome; it was to do, she felt, with some fairly disturbing emotions; it did not suggest contentment, but an aggressive energy, a dissatisfaction; there was a searching element, something that suggested pressures and difficulties she could not guess at. It was not an easy, amused face, like Ted's (Ted could even see the funny side of Barbara), but a watching, scowling face. Ruth wondered how old he was, and put him at about nineteen, but did not ask.

"I had these tickets. I just thought you might like it," he said.

"I've never been before. Not there," she said politely.

She had spent three hours wondering what to wear for the Zoo, and was attired much as he was, in cord jeans, a white sweater, and a leather jacket.

"You go up to London often?"

"Hardly ever. I suppose you know it quite well, if you're there all the term time?"

"Mm. Well enough."

"You—you live at home in the holidays?"

"No. I don't get on with my parents."

Ruth's heart sank a little, thinking how that would go down with her mother.

"I live with the parents of a friend of mine. A school-friend. He's pushed off now, and I have his room. They're easy. We get on all right."

"You were at school in Northend?"

"Yeah. I went to the Beehive. Where do you go?"

"Hanningham Comprehensive."

"I know it. We used to play them at soccer. We always beat 'em by miles."

"But we're good at soccer. We nearly always win."

"Well, we were better. We were top in the county three years running. That's when I was captain." He smiled, tentatively. "It's the only thing I ever liked at school."

"D'you still play?"

"No."

"That's a pity."

"Well, it doesn't go with what I do now. I can't. I just go swimming, that's all. You can't do much else in London. Are you any good at swimming?"

"Not much." Ruth, aware of her floundering breast-stroke, felt a qualm. Suppose he asked her? She was too skinny in a bathing costume anyway. "I ride," she said. "I'm not very sporty otherwise."

"What, a bike? Or do you mean a horse?"

"A horse. A pony, anyway. But he's good. He's won lots of rosettes—prizes, I mean."

"What for? Jumping?"

"Yes."

"Cripes, I've seen them on the 'telly.' The women, I mean. They must be as tough as hell. You one of those?"

"Not as good as them! I don't jump for England! Just the local Pony Club and things. But the pony's not fit at the moment—he's turned out."

"So you just do the gardening instead? You're always gardening."

Ruth felt herself go scarlet. But he wasn't teasing; she realized that he didn't know why she was always gardening. She was so relieved that she laughed.

"Well—riding's better. I miss him."

"The horse? What's it called?"

"Toadhill Flax. Toad."

"God Almighty, that's unkind."

"Yes. But that was it, when I had him. He was registered."

"Sounds like a perennial weed."

"I suppose it does."

The conversation closed, nothing else leading from it, and they both looked out of the window. Ruth saw fields and cows and woods, her eyes seeing but her brain registering nothing but a starry, unbelievable confusion, like a drawing in a comic of someone being knocked out. When the train stopped at the next station, he said, "That bloke in your house the other day—is he your brother?"

"Yes. Ted. He's married but he comes home quite often. He's got a new house in the village, but they're always having rows, him and Barbara. Have you got a brother? Or a sister?"

"No."

So he was what *Marybelle* called a "loner," always a particularly romantic figure in *Marybelle*. In fact, Ruth thought, it must be rather horrid, especially if he lived apart from his parents as well.

"What's wrong with your parents? They can't be *that* bad?"

"Oh, can't they?" he said darkly.

A qualm overlaid Ruth's eagerness, half compassion for him, half a jolting apprehension at seeing her mother's unspoken but strongly implied fears being borne out. All her mother's nice boys had exemplary parents, usually good friends of Ruth's mother and father. Satisfactory parents were one of the conditions of her mother's code. Unsatisfactory parents *and* probation . . . Ruth felt the cold breath, and steadfastly ignored it, grasping instead at the hopeful straws she felt might yield more credit.

"You must have done well at school to get to university."

"No. I got the sack," he said. "I was offered the scholarship the same day I got thrown out. It was a bit of a joke."

"What did they throw you out for?" Ruth tried to speak quite coolly, as if she knew a lot of people who had been sacked from school. She could see the proper word for it on her mother's lips: "Ex*pelled!*" and the expression that would accompany it.

"Something I did," he said, without elaboration. "But they couldn't take the scholarship away. I was laughing. I packed up school and I packed up my parents at the same time. The County gave me a grant. I hadn't really anything to complain about."

Ruth looked at him uncertainly. The thought of rejecting such authorities with the abandon he was suggesting awed her.

"Didn't you feel—sort of—on your own?"

"Better than with all that crowd on my back."

25

"But now—isn't it better? Isn't there anybody? Your parents——"

"Not my parents. That doesn't change. But it's all right, yes. There's the old friends when I'm down here, and a few at college during term, and my Prof. at college. He's all right. We get on. He bails me out when I'm in trouble."

"What, literally?"

He laughed. "If you like."

Ruth was glad of the laugh, for his eyes were sharp, as if he had guessed she was probing. Ruth, scared by pushing him, resolved to forget it. She had known, just as her mother had known, that he was no Gordon Hargreaves; she would choose to accept the revelations as proving his sincerity in not deceiving her, and his refreshing lack of self-pity, rather than as evidence of a doubtful background. But the starriness had gone; in its place there was something far less fictional, something very solid, in spite of being compounded of tenderness and compassion and all manner of delicate emotions, something that her mother was not going to move, bully as she might. Ruth had discovered Pat wasn't going to let her down. Whether because of or in spite of what he had said—and she didn't know which it was—she admired him even more ardently.

The train journey was over in what felt to Ruth like ten minutes, but was in fact fifty. They walked in silence down into the underground and Pat bought two tickets to Charing Cross. Ruth was puzzled by the destination, thinking that the Zoo was somewhere in Regent's Park, but she got obediently on to the Circle Line train and emerged eight stations later into a daylight that gave on to the Thames embankment. Pat led the way up a flight of steps that led from the pavement and up to the footbridge that crossed the Thames alongside the railway out of Charing Cross. On one side a plane tree reached out its sooty leaves, screening the traffic below, and on the other the electric trains racked towards the Kentish suburbs, uncomfortably close and noisy. Ruth, even more puzzled, saw the Thames glinting below in a doubtful sunlight, and a cruise steamer casting off for Greenwich. Between trains she hesitated.

"Where are we going?"

Pat looked at her in surprise. "There, of course," he said, pointing across the river. Ruth looked, and saw a large grey concrete building which she took at first to be something to do with the trains. "The Festival Hall."

"The Festival Hall?"

She was completely thrown. "But you said——" And she remembered that he hadn't said anything at all, only that he had tickets for something to do with his work.

"I thought——" She felt panic seize her, groping for some sort of a connection. For heaven's sake, what was the Festival Hall for? It wasn't a zoo. It was something rarefied and intelligent and serious . . . "Music, you mean?"

"Yes. Didn't I say?"

"You said it was to do with your work. I thought the Zoo."

He looked at her for a moment as if she had taken leave of her senses. Then, as if he had remembered, his face cleared and he laughed. He seemed to think it extraordinarily funny.

"Of course! I did say that—and the zoology. I'd forgotten. You thought we were going to the Zoo?"

"Yes, I did. What's so funny?"

"I'm sorry." But he was still laughing.

"What's this got to do with your work? I don't get it."

"My Prof. gave me the tickets. Did I say it was to do with my work? How could it possibly be to do with zoology?"

"Well, *you* said. I don't know." Ruth was put out, trying to adjust. It didn't hang together at all. "I don't see that music has anything to do with zoology at all. I wasn't expecting music."

"You don't mind?" he asked rather anxiously.

"No. I'm just surprised. I didn't expect . . ."

It was one of those contradictions again, completely baffling. The Festival Hall was classical sort of stuff surely? She could have understood if it was a pop concert. "What is it, this concert? An orchestra? That sort of thing?"

"Yes. Rachmaninov and Beethoven. Nothing way-out. You'll like it."

"But——" She looked at him doubtfully as they walked on, the tide ebbing far below, and the bridge trembling to the trains—"You mean *you* like it? You go often? It's not the first time?"

"No. I go quite often."

She had to rethink, reshuffle everything. As soon as she thought she knew one thing about him, he said something that undid it all. They were across the river and going down the steps on the other side, crossing the wide-paved concourse in front of the hall. It was the first thing she had learned about him that she could offer up to her mother proudly. "He likes classical music. We went to a concert." It was an impeccable way to spend a Sunday afternoon in London. After the shock had worn off, she felt very happy and pleased, keenly taking in the unfamiliar surroundings as they went up the steps and through the big glass doors. Inside she found that there was, curiously, a slight affinity with the Zoo after all; it was like a giant aviary, seeming to stretch up and out on all sides, with screens of glass and flights of apparently transparent, nebulous stairs, and people wandering everywhere, twittering and bobbing above and below, tropical Sunday finches . . . Ruth was intrigued.

"What a fantastic place! Where does the orchestra play?"

"In the concert hall. Not here. This is all extra, for milling about in beforehand, and afterwards. We've got three-quarters of an hour—we'll go and get something to eat first. There's a café overlooking the river. Okay?"

"Yes. Lovely."

She had never been taken out like this before. It was like a dream, a *Marybelle* story. She drifted along the self-service counter, taking sandwiches and coffee and a gooey, creamy sort of pie, and Pat paid and they sat at a table looking across towards the river. The café was fairly crowded, and to Ruth everyone looked peculiarly benign and civilized and well-dressed, and she blushed for her Zoo clothes, remembering how she thought she would have been spending the afternoon, looking at camels. And now this . . . and Beethoven, and someone she had never even heard of. She mustn't cough, and clap in the wrong places. She didn't know anything like that.

Pat ate his ham sandwiches and drank his coffee, and offered to fetch another coffee, which she refused. It seemed to Ruth that he had withdrawn somewhat, but she was so happy that she didn't mind. Once a boy about Pat's own age nodded to him as he passed, and Pat said, "Hey," without much interest. He did not gaze about him like Ruth, but sat staring into space. His expression did not suggest boredom, but rather preoccupation, almost anxiety, Ruth thought. He was contradicting himself again, the vital, aggressive element quite abruptly withdrawn into this brooding reverie.

Ruth, not wishing to interrupt, was perfectly content watching people going past with their trays. The place was fairly full, but her eye was caught by a striking girl in a long brown velvet coat coming towards where they were sitting, searching for an empty table. She was to Ruth's eyes unusually handsome, with a proud, confident carriage, a face with wide-spaced golden-brown eyes, delicate nervous nostrils and fine cheek-bones like an intellectual French film-star, and a stunning mane of bright chestnut hair. Ruth was not the only one admiring this vision, who was accompanied by an elegant youth in matching brown suede. The girl came down the aisle and to Ruth's astonishment stopped by their table and said, "Why, Pat!"

Pat looked up with a jerk, his expression reacting slowly, as if he had come from a long way away. Ruth looked jealously for the light of pleasure in his eye, but saw only a cautious surprise.

"Hullo," he said, very non-committal. And he nodded to the boy. "Hullo, Bob."

"Oh, of course!" the girl said. "We might have guessed you'd be here today! How long until——"

"It's six weeks yet," Pat said.

"How's it going?"

"Very well, thank you."

"No problems?"

"Of course. But nothing insoluble."

"Well, I wish you luck. You've got that Hampstead date all right, haven't you? You won't let me down?"

"No."

The golden-brown eyes came to Ruth and gave her a long, cool look. Ruth felt like a worm. The girl was beyond competing with; Ruth, for all her efforts, felt shabby, spotty, meagre, and worthless.

"See you then," said the vision, and wafted on her way to an empty table farther down.

Ruth looked at Pat.

"Who's she?"

"Her name's Clarissa."

"It would be," Ruth thought bitterly.

"She's at college. We work together sometimes. Come on —we'll go and take our seats. There's not long now."

He led the way out of the café, not amiable any more,

30

but silent and abstracted. As he had been silent and abstracted before Clarissa had interrupted them, Ruth could not fairly say that it was meeting Clarissa that had put him into this cool humor, but she had a feeling that meeting Clarissa hadn't improved anything for him. The idea of his *working* with Clarissa she would not dwell on; the vision of their two heads bent closely over a dissected monkey aroused qualms she would rather not experience.

But the atmosphere of the Festival Hall was too heady for her to dwell on these doubts, and her spirits rose as they climbed up the center stairs and threaded their way through the crowd to yet more stairs which appeared to Ruth to be more outside than in, with plane trees familiarly brushing the glass walls. Pat gave their tickets to a man who said, "Hullo, Pat," and Ruth said, "Do you live here or something?" and Pat said, "No, but I was a waiter for a month or two last year. I got to know people. Look, I'm sorry about these seats, if you've never been here before. You'll only see the violins."

Ruth saw what he meant when they sat down. They were in the front row, slightly to the left of the center, and the platform rose up in front of them so that their eye level coincided with the musicians' knees. As yet the platform was empty, and Ruth took in the vast pitch covered with music-stands and chairs, and the tiers of seats behind the platform, and the organ pipes beyond like some giant's toy convoluting into the dim recesses of the so-carefully designed ceiling, and turned round, and saw all the seats fanning away behind in the other direction, filling fast with the brightly plumaged Sunday people, and was excited in a most ridiculous childish fashion, in a most un-Clarissa-like, uncool bubbling way, which she felt obliged to cover up, with Pat so unimpressed beside her. She didn't have to show what a yokel she was.

Pat showed her the program. After a Rossini overture,

there was the Piano Concerto No. 2 by Rachmaninov and the Symphony No. 8 by Beethoven. It conveyed nothing to her at all. The members of the orchestra were now taking their seats, and getting out their instruments, but Ruth was puzzled by what appeared to be an enormous oversight on the part of the management, and could not restrain herself from inquiring:

"How can there be a piano concerto when there's no piano?"

"They bring it on, just before, and take it away afterwards," Pat said.

Ruth blushed. Not only was she a yokel, she was a stupid yokel.

She supposed, having seen it on the television, it should have been familiar enough, but to Ruth it was entrancing, listening to "The Thieving Magpie," and considering the violinists' feet, their socks in various shades of grey and their black shoes, and lifting her eyes to the wonderfully eloquent gestures of their right arms, all flowing together, the little fingers stretched in a way that made her long to be drawing: the black shapes and the white decorations of the fingers, and the golden intricacies of the line of violins, giving out a splendor that was entirely divorced and apart from the complete ordinariness of each individual player, who were the sort of men one saw everywhere, in shops and on the train, doing the crossword, washing the car on Sunday mornings, and taking the dog for a walk. When it was over, dissolved into warm, swelling applause, Ruth remarked on this strange paradox to Pat, and he said, "But it's only work, to them. To pay their mortgages and buy their cars."

"There must be more to it than that! Art——"

"Art is eighty-five per cent work," Pat said. "Hard work." He seemed very sure of this fact, speaking with a vehemence that suggested a personal, somewhat bitter experience.

"Even for him," he said, when the piano had duly made its appearance and was installed in place, and the soloist had followed the conductor on and was taking a quick introductory bow. "It's his work."

Ruth had always rather thought it was a gift. But when the anticipatory hush fell and the soloist wiped his hands nervously on his knees and the conductor raised his baton, she felt a lurch of compassion for his terrible responsibility, before all these people, to hit the right notes—the loneliness of it was appalling. There were surely, she thought, easier ways to pay the mortgage than this? And then his hands came down and played the first broken chords, and it was so fluid and effortless that her anxiety instantly slipped away. Softly at first, and then with an increasing urgency, the chords led the way into a deep turbulent melody. Ruth saw the violinists before her lift their bows, the conductor raise his baton with a tense white expectancy, holding in leash the whole gamut of poised breath and suspended finger until the exact, perfect moment when the solo piano could be resisted no longer, and they were launching on this eager, rhythmic tide which the piano had prepared for them. Ruth, having expected difficulties and incomprehension, was launched along with them, a drowning twig on the breast of flowing waters. Work it might be to them, but to Ruth, completely new to such a happening, it was an overwhelmingly emotional experience which she had no wish nor will to resist. She could not have put into words the effect it had on her; she only knew that in the slow movement she cried, and in the finale she cried again, but she was so happy it was crying for God knew what. Ruth didn't know. But in the crashing uproar of the applause afterwards, she was comforted to see that the soloist, bowing and shaking hands with the conductor, looked almost as shaken as she felt, although what emotion was prompting him she was not qualified to guess at. If it was only work, after all, it could have been pure relief.

She turned to ask Pat, but he was withdrawn in such a way that Ruth had a strange feeling that he was scarcely there at all. But when the appreciation had died down, and everyone had bowed for the last time, he turned to her, and Ruth felt that she was actually seeing him come back from this other world he was inhabiting; it was almost a physical thing, the eyes focusing on her almost with surprise, the mouth easing into the suggestion of a smile, a warming, a softening . . . Ruth was confirmed in her suspicion that Pat was a highly complex animal, a study on his own, well oriented in his zoology school.

"We'll go and get a drink," he said, very prosaic.

It was the interval, and most people were leaving the hall. They joined the throng, Ruth still not quite sure that her feet were on the ground. Her leaping happiness—all that and Pat too—was dangerous in its intensity. One could only fall from such heights. She tried to temper the mood, but it kept escaping, singing into the firmaments like the Rachmaninov melodies.

"What will you have?" Pat asked.

It was a bar, and Ruth had no idea what to ask for. She had a panicky glance around, but everyone had anonymous brown stuff that was no help to her.

"Coke," she said, and Pat took it without a qualm, and ordered coke and half a pint of bitter. They took their glasses and retreated, guarding them carefully in the crush. Coming towards them, *en route* for the bar and, regrettably, unavoidable, was the magnificent Clarissa.

"Oh, Pat! What did you think of it? I'm sorry to say it wearies me to death. *So* hackneyed. I wonder you can face the prospect at all. If I were you I'd——"

34

"You're *so* encouraging," Pat said, without smiling. "If I were you, I'd stop worrying about what you suppose are other people's difficulties and worry about your own. Your Hampstead date, for instance."

"Our Hampstead date," she corrected.

"Well, I'm not worried about my part in that. You should be, from what I last heard."

Although Ruth had no idea what they were talking about, she could see that Pat was being offensive. Clarissa's eyes went cold.

"You don't change, do you, Pat? I thought at one time we were civilizing you quite nicely. But I was wrong obviously."

She drifted away into the crowd with impeccable majesty. The suede Bob, following, gave Pat a sympathetic, eye-rolling grimace. Pat grinned.

He said to Ruth, "She should have been an actress," and the subject was closed, Ruth could see. She longed to ask questions, but Pat's expression forbade it. It was grim again and Ruth hated Clarissa for her interference.

"That music we heard—is it hackneyed?" she asked nervously. "I thought it was beautiful."

"It's both," Pat said.

"Hackneyed and beautiful?"

"Yes. Hackneyed only means it's played a lot, so that a lot of people know it, and what's wrong with that?"

"I knew it," she said. "That beginning—and that slow bit. It was quite familiar to me."

"Yes. The first time I heard it, I was just little. My mother took me to the pictures to see some crummy film about a housewife who fell in love with a doctor. Every time they were looking into each other's eyes, or thinking about each other on the railway platform—the slow movement came on and all the women in the cinema wept. They all came out looking as if they'd been to a funeral. But my mother said it was lovely. It was Rachmaninov that did it, not the director."

"Those old films . . . it's only animals dying that make me cry, like *My Friend Flicka*. I think I've seen that film—something about an encounter. The title, I mean. I remember the railway station too, and at the end, she goes home, back to her husband, and leaves the doctor for ever, and she goes in at the door, and the music plays——"

"The coda—and everybody cries——"

"Yes. That's it. I remember. My mother cried too. It was a very sad film, all that parting for ever."

"Well, I don't remember. Only the music."

"It must be awful."

"What?"

"Parting for ever."

"Oh. Yes. And never coming. Someone you expect never coming." He said it in a way that suggested he knew. Ruth was silent, caught by a wrenching of her feelings, half compassion, half jealousy, that stopped her voice. Keyed up by the music, moved by a sympathy towards someone stronger than she had ever experienced, she looked at him over the top of her glass, and found him regarding her with equal gravity. The mutual contemplation was undisturbed by the surrounding crush; Ruth felt that they were perfectly alone.

"What's your name?" he asked, never having asked before.

"Ruth."

"And then we came out and walked across the river and had tea in a place, and then we walked some more, into Trafalgar Square or somewhere, and the church bells were ringing . . ."

Ruth had nothing to hide from her mother. Telling her,

it was like saying poetry, savoring the image behind the words, the fountains blown by a cool evening breeze and the starlings' chatter and the gusty din of the bells of St. Martin's pounding off the walls of Duncannon Street, and Pat walking with his hands in his pockets past the Sunday shouters and the American tourists and herself at his elbow in this trance-like state of unclouded bliss, which had continued right from Rachmaninov to the parting at the railway station.

"So you've got him all wrong," she said passionately to her mother. "And he never even touched me either," she added. "Not like Gordon Hargreaves."

Mrs. Hollis laughed, in spite of herself. "Well, I must say, I'm flabbergasted. A classical concert! You mean Beethoven sort of thing?"

"Yes. It was Beethoven actually. And that piano thing by Rachmaninov that was in that film where the housewife fell in love with the doctor, and went back to her husband and you cried——"

"*Brief Encounter*? Oh, that was a beautiful film! They don't make films like that now! Really, is that what you heard? That was beautiful!"

Her husband said darkly, "Why did you cry, if the housewife went back to her husband?"

"It was so real," said Mrs. Hollis dreamily. "She was just an ordinary housewife, not young and pretty, but just ordinary and dull, and she met this doctor, and he wasn't dazzlingly handsome either, just nice and kind, and they fell in love—fantastically in love, not just a passing thing—but she went back to her husband . . . she went in at the door and he was just sitting there, homely and ordinary. She couldn't leave him, you see. He had never done anything wrong, or hurt her, and she went back, and that was the end of the film."

"It sounds fantastically old-fashioned," Ruth said.

"Oh, yes, I've no doubt. Nowadays she'd have moved in with the doctor, and two families would have been completely wrecked in order that she could fulfil herself, or whatever. There's a lot to be said for being old-fashioned, my girl."

"Yes," said Ruth, and dreamed her way up to bed.

"That's a good old-fashioned thing that's afflicting Ruth now," Mr. Hollis said to his wife when she had gone. "Even I'm not so homely and ordinary as to remain unaware of the fact that the girl has got it very badly. Your plan miscarried, my dear."

"What plan?"

"You said that if she got to know him a little better, he was bound to prove that he had feet of clay. Not so, obviously. He's the Angel Gabriel as far as she's concerned."

"Well, I must say—again—you could knock me down with a feather. I just put him down as a typical lout. I've never seen him smile, or say thank you, or say anything at all, come to that. He flings the loaf at you and drives off like a maniac. He's a strapping great lad, built like a longshoreman, hair all over his collar. Although he's got nice hands, come to think of it. The only thing that looks even faintly artistic about him. Long fingers and well-kept nails. But the Festival Hall! No, quite the last thing I would have imagined."

"Encouraging, I would have said."

"Possibly. But I'm not convinced. I'd like to know a little more about him."

"In a place like this," her husband said, "I wouldn't think that would take you long."

Chapter Three

✸

Pat glowered at Mrs. Hollis, handing in a large uncut. "Five uncut. Fifty-five pence," he said.

Mrs. Hollis handed him a note, and he scooped about in his money-bag for the change. Mrs. Hollis decided that his neck and his hair were clean, and it was only the clothes that made him look scruffy. And he was working after all. She hadn't the nerve to ask him any questions; there was this block, that Ruth presumably had overcome, this aggressive reserve, as if he was behind a barbed-wire fence.

"Ten, twenty." He counted out her change, hesitated. "Tell Ruth—tell her I'll be in the Big Top tomorrow night at seven."

"Where and what is the Big Top, might I ask?"

"It's a coffee-bar on the front. She'll know it."

"I take it that's an invitation?"

"I'm working. I can't take her out. I just want to see her."

"Very well. I'll tell her. I don't know what her plans are." She paused. "You seem to work very hard."

"I work in a pub Saturday nights. But I can see her first."

"All right."

He slouched off down the drive, whistling. Mrs. Hollis smiled to herself. Ruth, back at school for the last fortnight of term, had not seen Pat since her day out with him but had inquired after him every day, with an increasing despair. It was for her sake that Mrs. Hollis smiled, against her better judgement. She thought, if she saw Mrs. Pargeter, she would ask her a few more questions, although it wasn't really something she cared to do. But if this friendship was on . . . the probation thing worried her.

"I don't know if you can call it taking you out," she said to Ruth when she came home. "Pretty casual, I call it."

But Ruth, after the agony of the past week, glowed like a spark in the wind.

"Oh, it's lovely! I thought——" But it had been only too plain what she had been thinking. It had been a week like a year, bereft of her gardening sessions, and the daily blessing of merely seeing Pat. She had dreamed of him all day and all night.

"Well, if you think it's worth going all that way for half an hour in a coffee-bar . . ." But it could as well have been Cornwall, or twice as far. Mrs. Hollis decided to save her breath.

Ruth went on the bus, which was supposed to get into the bus station at seven o'clock exactly. Running, she would be at the Big Top at three minutes past seven. It was a terrible risk, in her eyes, but her whole family, Ted included, had derided the idea of her going on the bus before —the three o'clock—merely in order to be there punctually. "He'll wait three minutes, dear, if he loves yer," Ted said. But Ruth kept remembering what he had said, about someone not coming. And then, sternly, "But he doesn't think of me like that—not yet. That was someone who mattered." Mattered terribly, she thought. And she went into another of her dreams, about him being crossed in love, which lasted her all the way to Northend. She got off the bus, feeling sick and unreal, and ran all the way to the coffee-bar, only stopping three yards short of the door. It was no good trying to look as if it didn't matter. She had no breath, not just through running, but through everything. She had bursting stitch, and an agony of mind that was a hundred times sharper than anything physical. She went in, white and shaking.

He was sitting at a table in the window. He had a tie on and a white shirt, and looked quite normal. She went over to him and sat down and stared at him.

"Pat."

"Hullo," he said. He gave a very slight smile. "I thought your mother might not pass the message on."

"Oh, she's not that bad."

"No. I wondered if you'd think it was worth it. I have to go to work in half an hour. I thought you might be in Northend anyway, so I mentioned it."

"She said that. Yes, of course I thought it was worth it."

"Oh, well." He smiled. "That's all right."

Ruth smiled, all the pains dissolving. It was worth it already.

"What'll you have?"

"Just a coffee." She didn't want to be interrupted by food. He ordered two coffees from the waitress, and considered her again.

"Why do you have to work so hard?" she said.

"I do just now. Later it will be all right. I'm sorry, because—well, the other things have to go. Like tonight. We could have gone down the pier or something."

Out of the window the sea was bathed in a calm pink evening light. The tide was out and the pier marched out over the shining mud on spidery legs; the fairy lights were on and summer couples were walking hand in hand; Ruth could feel the echoing boards under her feet and smell the sea and hear the hollow slapping of it far below. Her longing to walk there with Pat made her quiver.

"I wish we could!" And then, hastily, "But it's all right. I mean if the work's important——"

"It's five quid tonight in the pub, and I can't pass it up

41

anyway—he'd go raving. Tomorrow I work all day—study, that is—and then it's the bread again. The bread's only part-time, but all the same I'm going to pack it in soon. I'd rather have an evening job, and do my own work in the morning. I must have more time for it."

"How long have you got to do at university? Aren't you nearly finished?"

"I've got another year. I've only told you this to explain —about not going out. I'm not complaining or anything. But if it's a waste of time for you——" He shrugged. "You live so far out."

"Where do you live?"

"Fiddler's End."

"That's just as far out."

"We've arranged things badly. Or if I had some transport . . . Well, that's how it is."

"Hey, mind if I butt in?" Somebody stopped by the table. Ruth looked up and saw a sharply-dressed boy with a cheerful quick face. "How's things, Penn? Long time no see."

"Cripes, Maxwell, get lost," Pat said, but quite amiably, so that Maxwell sat down, and looked with unconcealed interest at Ruth.

"That's Ruth," Pat said. "Maxwell."

"Pleased to meet you," said Maxwell.

Ruth tried to look more gracious than she felt. "Hullo."

"Hul*lo*." Maxwell gave her a dazzling smile, and said to Pat, "How's the old——"

"Very well, thank you," Pat said. "How's the car trade?"

"It isn't, unfortunately. I've lost my license for twelve months—the old breath, you know. A hundred and God knows how many milli-whatsits. Green as a cucumber. So I'm working in the stores until I get it back. Dead boring. You on the old stint tonight?"

"Yeah, eight o'clock."

"Don't you ever let up?"

"It's a good job, this one."

"All those sweaty trippers in their cups. What's Ruth going to do then—come out with Uncle Maxwell?"

"No fear," Ruth said.

"We could take a stroll, and then call on Penn and see him at work, and take a noggin with him between 'Nellie Dean' and 'Home Sweet Home.' Not agreeable?"

The thought of seeing Pat again later attracted Ruth.

Pat said, "I'd trust you with him, I think."

"Where is this pub then?"

"Just down the road a bit. The Jolly Sailor."

Ruth knew the Jolly Sailor. It was a huge modern pub which attracted the Saturday night trippers and was always cramful and very rowdy. It was quite a different proposition from the Royal Festival Hall, something she would definitely not want to tell her mother about. Pat glanced at his watch.

"I ought to be going. Shall I see you later?"

"Yes," said Ruth.

"That's my girl," said Maxwell.

Ruth looked anxiously at Pat, and he gave her a reassuring wink. "He's okay. Aren't you, Maxwell?" he added, ominously.

"Straight as a die," said Maxwell.

Pat got up. "See you later then."

Ruth watched him depart, anxious and excited. She had no feelings either for or against Maxwell; he was of interest entirely for what light he could throw on Pat.

"Why do you call him Penn?" she asked.

"It's what we called him at school. Pennington."

"Is that his name? Pennington? You were at school together?"

"Yes."

The waitress came, and Maxwell ordered sausage and chips, and asked her what she wanted. Now that there was time to waste, she asked for a coffee and a chocolate éclair. Maxwell, she thought, knew all the reasons why Pat was as he was, all the things she wanted to know, but—because of Pat's own reserve—she was wary of asking. It was going down to Mrs. Pargeter's level, prying and nosing. If Pat wanted her to know the story of his life, he would tell her, no doubt, in his own good time. But, having made this noble resolution, her curiosity was too much for her.

"What was he like at school?"

"What was he like?" Maxwell looked slightly baffled. "The same as all the rest of us, I suppose, pretty bloody awful. He was always in trouble, probably worse than anybody else. He asked for it, mind you. He never did a stroke of work. Soccer was the only thing he was keen on. He was a wizard on the field. We were hardly ever beaten—in fact never, the last year. I was in the team too—we had some good times. I still play, but he's packed it in. Had to, I suppose. Pity."

"How come he got a scholarship, if he never worked?"

"Oh, he worked in that. He was superb, a natural—nobody was a bit surprised that Prof. bloke taking him up. And since then he's never stopped working. I don't know how he keeps it up. The only holiday he's ever had in three years—we all told him this but I don't think he appreciated the joke—was when he was in jail for three months last summer."

Ruth felt as if he had hit her. It was fate's own reward for prying, a cold, sick turning over in her stomach.

Maxwell looked at her and said, "Oh, cripes, have I said too much? Forget it, for God's sake. I wasn't thinking. It wasn't anything much."

"What was it?"

"Look, I'm not getting on the wrong side of Penn. You ask him if you want to know. Let's forget it. A slip of the tongue. I'll just get outside the old sausage and chips and then we'll take the air. I take it you're very much struck? I don't know how he does it, without even trying. The last bird he had—oh, cripes, something else we'd better not talk about. That's old history. Don't you worry. He's all right— had a lot to contend with, you know. You haven't met his parents? No, well, try not to. Although I don't think he has anything to do with them now. Tell me about you. Penn's terribly lucky in lots of ways, having a girl like you, mainly. How did you meet him?"

Ruth told him. She was as glad to be talking about herself as Maxwell was for the subject to be changed. After the shock, Ruth found that she just wanted to forget it. She didn't want to know. Her curiosity was cured. She talked eagerly, covering up the abyss that had yawned beneath her feet for that awful moment: therapeutic small talk that was as necessary as air. When Maxwell had finished they went out and walked along the prom, and Maxwell told her all about the car trade, and the night he had got caught out with the breathalyzer and, although it was all so boring, she latched on to it gratefully and made all the right encouraging remarks, while the sun went down over the sea like a great red flower and the sharpness of dusk nipped bare arms and legs. The arcades and cafés and pubs on the other side of the road were filling up fast. Maxwell glanced at his watch.

"Old Penn's been going an hour. We'll go and pay a visit. Not that he's allowed much let-up till closing time, mind you . . ."

They crossed the road. Ruth knew that her last bus home went in ten minutes' time, and she knew equally well that she wasn't going to be on it. Beyond that she would not think. There was a terrible noise of drunken singing coming out of the Jolly Sailor. She steeled herself against her upbringing, and followed closely on Maxwell's heels, passing from the coolness of the sea air into a hot, sweating riot of humanity. The crush at the bar was appalling.

"Hey, don't get lost," Maxwell said. "Stay with me. What'll you have. A Martini? What do you like?"

"Coke," Ruth said.

"What, are you sure?"

"Yes." She was looking for Pat, but could not see him. The bar was the longest she had ever seen, and there were about a dozen barmen, but no Pat.

"Where is he?"

"Over there, of course," Maxwell said. He jerked his head towards the noisiest and most crowded end of the room, where a great rowdy phalanx of middle-aged men and women were singing "Red Sails in the Sunset" to an accomplished but invisible piano accompaniment. Ruth, shoved and trodden on, backed out, not wanting beer all over her best dress. She didn't understand, but had to wait for Maxwell. He came, holding the glasses above his head.

"Can you get through?" he bawled at her, nodding once more in the direction of the singing. "We might get a seat if anyone's moving out."

Ruth went unwillingly.

"We haven't got to sing, have we? What a terrible place! Where is Pat?"

"He's playing the piano."

"He's what?" Ruth thought she was hearing things.

"At the piano, of course. What else do you think he's doing?"

Ruth stared at Maxwell's surprised face, pressed willy-nilly about six inches from her own. He had three glasses clutched under his chin.

46

"I've got him a beer, if he can get away for five minutes."

"Did you say he was playing the piano?"

"Yes. What's wrong? Shove on a bit and we'll tell him we've arrived."

But Ruth was rooted to the ground. The piano, unlike most pub pianos, was being played with a finesse that even she recognized. The knowledge that this was Pat at work was the biggest contradiction yet, like being hit on the head with the keyboard. She stared at Maxwell.

He said, "Don't tell me he hasn't even told you that? What he does? When did you two meet? Tonight?"

"What does he do?"

"He's a student at the something college—can't remember which one—of music. Playing the old pianner."

"He said zoology," Ruth said faintly.

"He said what?" yelled Maxwell.

"Zoology," she shouted back.

"You mean I've put my foot in it again? Zoology? Where did he dream that up? All this work he does then—what did you think it was? Looking at elephants under a microscope?"

"Yes. Sort of—I thought——"

"Cripes, he's been having you on! I'll tell him, the old fraud! You haven't even heard him play before? Well, I can tell you, make the most of this, because it's usually the old Beethoven touch, dead gloomy, not decent stuff like this. He only does this for bread and butter. Shove on, girl. Let's go and tip this beer down his neck."

Ruth shoved on, in a daze. She put her shoulder between two fat men immediately in front of her, and wedged them apart. "Steady on, ducks," said one of them, yielding, and she fell through and found herself at Pat's shoulder.

"Give 'm some room, darling," said a face in hers.

"We've brought you a beer, Penn," Maxwell said, arriving with force, and with the drinks miraculously intact.

"Thanks," said Pat. "I'm ready for one."

He had launched into a current sentimental ballad which his admirers were taking up with deafening fervor. Ruth, resisting the crush behind her to give him room, gazed down at his fingers on the keyboard, mesmerized by this turn of events. She saw the scab on the side of his right forefinger, and the episode of the sticking-plaster suddenly made sense. How dim she was not to have guessed! After the Festival Hall—only an imbecile would have failed to see a connection.

"She thought you studied elephants for a living," Maxwell was saying cheerfully. Ruth felt herself going crimson. "What have you been telling her?"

"Just move your solar plexus out of the way, you fool," Pat said.

"You're a fraud, Penn. Always were. She's far too good for you. I'll take you on, Ruth—I'll give you a break. I'm worth six of this long-haired, tinkling virtuoso——"

"I'll take *you* on when I get to the end of this," Pat said.

The fervent, beer-washed voice of the singing crowd rose up in maudlin crescendo, and Ruth watched his fingers go up the keys in a running scale so fast that she could hardly follow them, then down in a complicated progression of chords to a thunderous conclusion.

"A touch of the old Rachmaninov," he said, reaching for his beer. "That's to please the old man here," he added. "If I just strum he gives me three quid, but if I give the old master touch, he gives me a fiver. He considers it adds class to the place."

He got up. "Let's get a breath of air."

"Don't be long, darling," said an anxious woman.

"Five minutes," he said.

They pushed their way out to a place near the open door,

and Pat leaned against the wall and wiped his face with a handkerchief. He had pulled his tie loose and Ruth could see the trickles of sweat down his neck.

"I don't think this was a very good idea," he said to her. "You coming to this place."

"It was a lovely idea," Maxwell said. "Speak for yourself."

"I don't mind," Ruth said. "Why did you tell me zoology?"

Pat grinned.

Maxwell said, "He's afraid of his image. Doesn't want to be thought a pansy. That's it, isn't it, Penn?"

Pat said to him, "Go and get me another pint. It's on the house. Get rid of him for five minutes," he said to Ruth.

Maxwell went, quite cheerful.

"People have funny ideas about pianists," Pat said. "Think you're just a layabout or something."

"I think it's marvellous," Ruth said. Jostled from behind, she squeezed in beside Pat, against the wall. His shoulder was hard against hers. "I thought, last week—well, I should have guessed. I'm a bit slow. You said it was for your work."

"Yes. I'm working on that concerto now."

"Is that what you do, after the bread round?"

"Practice. Yes."

"You've got a piano where you live?"

"No. There's one in the village hall they let me use. It's quite a good one."

"What, you have the place to yourself?"

"Except clinic afternoons, and the chiropodist and things."

"Then what happens?"

"I just carry on. They don't mind, only if I'm on scales or just working on a few phrases they keep interrupting and asking for 'a proper piece,' which is a bit annoying. It's like Housewife's Choice. The old ladies always want 'Abide with Me'."

He turned and smiled at her. The top of her head was on a level with his upper lip. She noticed he had a scar on his lip, and nice teeth, and she realized that he didn't smile very often, which was why she had never noticed his teeth before.

"They're not keen on Rachmaninov cadenzas."

He finished off his pint, and Maxwell came back with another.

"Your blonde girl-friend wants you back," Maxwell said. "She wants you to play 'Smoke Gets in Your Eyes.' Just about her vintage, I should have said."

"Never 'eard of it," Pat said. Maxwell offered him a cigarette, which he refused. He offered Ruth one and she shook her head.

"How are you going to get home?" Pat said to her. "What time's your last bus?"

"It's gone."

"I'll walk her home," Maxwell said with an optimistic leer.

"It's twelve miles," Pat said.

"I was joking, of course!"

"If you stay till I've finished, I can get the bread van," Pat said. "I can't think of anything else. Can you?"

"No," Ruth said. "Only hitch-hike."

"On a Saturday night, out of this place! That would be asking for it. I must get back—there's the boss wondering why the lovely silence. He wants blood, that man."

He straightened up and looked rather anxiously at Ruth. "I won't be away till half-past eleven. That all right?"

"Yes. Of course."

When he had gone Maxwell said, "He's getting terribly civilized in his old age. Not the fellow he was at all. Shall we take a toddle outside? Bit of fresh air and all that?"

"Why, what was he like before?"

"He wasn't so polite. He said more. You get the feeling now he's being very careful. What's it to be then? A turn down the pier? It's a bit late for a film. Or another noggin farther down?"

Ruth chose the pier, but there was no magic in it with Maxwell. The magic was in her head; she was trying to sort it all out again, turning Pat into a pianist. She wanted Maxwell to talk about Pat, but was sensitive enough to appreciate that Maxwell would rather talk about himself. While he talked, she disentangled fragments that had to be re-thought: Clarissa, for example, did not study monkeys under a microscope, but played duets with Pat, an enviably intimate association that Ruth preferred not to dwell on. There was only one point about the revelation that she felt moved to offer to Maxwell:

"I would never have thought . . . you know, you think musicians are sort of—different. Frightfully intellectual and —and superior——" But then she remembered the grey socks of the orchestra in the Festival Hall, and Pat saying it was all for paying their mortgages, making that celestial noise. "He treats it just like an ordinary job."

Maxwell said, "But it is, to him. What else would he have done? If he hadn't taken it up he would have had to go and work in some dead-end job like the rest of us—like the bread round. Who wants to do that every day? He might work very hard practicing now, but he knows that, with luck, he might get somewhere—he'll earn a lot of money, and travel, and meet people, and people will admire him. Well, that's not bad, is it? Worth trying. More than most of us will ever aspire to. He's got it all worked out pretty carefully, and he thinks it's worth the effort. It was either that, or just get a job down here, earning the old pittance for your forty-hour week. He never put on airs about it that I remember. At school, it was just something he did, like other people did metalwork or the girls did typing. And he hasn't changed in that, at all."

They went back to the Jolly Sailor at closing time, and waited for Pat, braced among the extremely cheerful streams of departing guests. He came gratefully, looking very hot and tired.

"Thank God that's over for another week."

They went outside and Maxwell said, "If you're getting the van, Penn, you could drop me off too."

"Yeah, if you like."

They walked up the street, Ruth in the middle. Maxwell was talking to Pat about someone she didn't know, and Pat walked along saying "Yes" at intervals, and yawning. They turned off the Parade down the side street to the bakery, and it was quiet and cool. Pat stopped under a street lamp and pulled some keys out of his pocket.

"There's a couple of coppers coming this way," Maxwell said quietly. "Is this okay with——"

"Oh, cripes, of course," Pat said.

Ruth looked at him, the sharp memory recurring. She felt herself shiver involuntarily. They came up to the gates of the bakery yard and Pat got out the key. The two policemen crossed the road and came towards them. Maxwell said something that Ruth didn't catch and Pat swore, softly but forcefully.

"You live here?"

The policemen had stopped behind them. Pat opened the door and turned around.

"I work here."

Ruth, watching him, saw him stiffen into an attitude of belligerent defiance that was a shock to her law-abiding soul. He stood in the gateway, the contempt so apparent on his face that it was almost an assault in itself. Ruth was frightened, more by Pat than by the police.

"What's your name?" asked one of the policemen.

"Ask Mitchell. He knows it," Pat said curtly, jerking his head at the speaker's colleague.

"I asked you," said the policeman.

Pat hesitated.

Maxwell said, "His name is Patrick Pennington."

"That correct?" the policeman asked Pat.

"Yes."

"Funny time to start work, isn't it?"

Pat said, "We're getting a van out, if you want to know, to drive home in." He opened the palm of his hand and showed a car-key lying in it. "It's the van I drive every day. It's allowed. It's one of the perks of the job. Ask Mr. Simmonds, the manager."

"Show me your driving license," said the policeman.

Pat groped in his back pocket and pulled it out. The policeman took it and studied it intently, and passed it to Mitchell. He glanced at Mitchell and raised an eyebrow.

"All right?"

"Seems in order." He sounded reluctant.

"It *is* in order," Pat said.

"Watch it," said the first policeman.

Ruth saw Maxwell touch Pat's shoulder, an urgent needling of the forefinger. Pat stood rigid, waiting for his license. Mitchell, a sharp-featured man with a close hair cut and hard eyes, leafed it through again and handed it back, unsmiling.

"All right.

"Thank *you*," Pat said.

The two policemen walked on. Pat flung open the door of the bakery yard.

"Oh, cripes!" he said. "Mitchell—the swine——!" His voice shook, the self-control he had evidently exercised during the brief questioning spilling into sharp and lurid epithets to describe Mitchell. The underlying violence frightened Ruth; it was a far stronger passion than she had ever met in her own polite circle.

Maxwell was grinning. "I thought you were going to get yourself busted again. That's why I told them your name. You want a keeper, Penn, asking for it like that! You know with Mitchell you've only got to lift your hand to scratch your nose and he's got you for threatening behavior——"

"Oh, don't tell me!" Pat turned away towards the row of vans. "I know all about that beggar——"

"Who's Mitchell?" Ruth asked Maxwell, when Pat was out of earshot.

"He's the copper that had it in for Penn when he was still at school. He's one of those—you get to know 'em—they go by the book. They'll get you for anything. And Penn's allergic to policemen anyway, even the uncle types, let alone the beasts like Mitchell. It's his upbringing." He grinned again, as if it was all quite funny.

Pat drove the van through the gates and they closed them and locked them behind him, and climbed into the van. Ruth felt scrambled and cold, the fear still swinging in her stomach.

"It's all right?" she said to Pat. "They——"

"It's all right now," he said. "We're not supposed to use the vans, but if they'd called up Simmonds he'd have said it was all right. Then afterwards he'd have given me the sack. Might still, if they check on it. Not that I care."

His face by the street-lamps was taut and angry.

"Don't get into trouble for me," Ruth said. "I can still get a bus as far as——"

"It's all right." His voice was sharp. Ruth sat back, silenced.

"Have a bun," Maxwell said affably, from the back of the van. He passed over a brick-like doughnut.

"Thank you, I'm not that hungry," Ruth said.

They came out on to the arterial, and Pat put his foot down.

"How's your speedometer?" Maxwell murmured from the back. "Speaking from experience, of course."

"Seeing Mitchell's ugly face like that is shock enough to sober anybody."

"Yeah, but use your loaf, Penn. He'd love to run you in. You jolly nearly gave him the chance just now."

"Cripes, I'd like to give *him* three months!"

He pulled out and overtook a row of saloon cars, the speedometer flickering on sixty. Ruth watched the road ahead and the stab of the headlights, remembering that Pat did it every day and knew it well, and presumably knew what was beyond the limit of the lights. The emotions now were painful and mixed, the early sweetness trampled. Having learned so much about Pat in the last few hours, she decided she could well have done without the last episode. She did not like Pat's present bitterness. It fitted in too vividly with the picture of him which she wanted to forget, the picture Maxwell had raised over the cup of coffee. The bit she wouldn't mention to her mother.

As they bumped down the lane to the Hollis cottage, with Maxwell still eating doughnuts in the back, Pat's profile softened slightly, and he turned to Ruth and said, "I'm sorry about this. It wasn't much of an evening for you."

"It's all right," Ruth said. "Honestly."

"I hope you're not too late."

"No." Ruth hoped so too. The light was still on downstairs.

"I'll see you again."

But he didn't say when. He turned into her drive and braked, and leaned over and opened the door for her. His hair brushed her cheek.

"I'm sorry," he said again.

"It's all right," she repeated.

Maxwell, climbing into her vacated seat, said, "Good night, Ruth."

"Good night. And thank you."

She walked up the long drive, very slowly, listening to the van drive away up the lane. Now, the moment he had gone, she felt an agony of longing for him to be there again. It was so sharp she had to stop in the middle of the drive, unable to face her parents with this empty, demented feeling draining all the sense out of her. She stood and looked up at the sky through the pear-trees, lifting her face and feeling the coolness of the breeze that came off the river. It occurred to her, quite inappropriately, that once these strange feelings had been to do with ponies and winning something very special, the times when she had looked at the sky and been filled with inexplicable longings. It was the only thing she had to compare this present ache with. And now, remembering, every inexplicable longing she had ever experienced in the past was as nothing at all compared to this crushing sense of desolation at Pat's going.

"Ruth, are you there?"

Her mother was standing at the kitchen door. Ruth heard her voice and started walking again.

"Are you mad?" her mother said. "I heard the car go off ages ago. How can you take so long to walk up the drive? Some of us want to go to bed tonight."

"I'm not stopping you," Ruth said.

"Dear Ruth," her mother said ominously, "you are stopping me."

"Oh, I'm sorry, but he didn't finish till half-past eleven. We came straight home then. You aren't cross?"

"We—ll. Not now, I suppose." She sighed. "One worries —the Saturday night roads . . . Do you want a cup of tea?" She yawned.

"No. It doesn't matter. Do you know, he's a pianist!"

"Zoology, you said. What do you mean? He plays for a hobby?"

"No. It's what he's a student of. The zoology was just a joke. He plays the piano *fantastically*."

"Good gracious, you do surprise me! He doesn't look— well, what do pianists look like? I don't really know. Not like that, I'm sure. Really? Yes, that *is* a surprise, I must say."

Ruth was gratified to notice that the surprise was a pleasant one, judging by her mother's face. Pianists were, she supposed, eminently respectable—but, even in this generalization, Pat was a contradiction. The other things she had found out she did not mention.

"Are you seeing him again?" Mrs. Hollis asked, almost as if she was quite keen.

"Yes," Ruth said quietly. "Oh yes."

And she went to bed and prayed that she had spoken the truth.

Chapter Four

✦

Ruth did not see Pat all the next week, and he left no message. When, having broken up for the summer holidays, she arrived home on Friday, she missed him by five minutes. It was a hot, cloudless day. Having run all the way from the bus-stop, she could have wept when her mother said:

"He was early today."

Ruth ate her lunch in silence. Her mother watched her without saying anything. When she had finished, Ruth went upstairs and changed into her old jeans and pink gingham shirt, did her eyes with great care, tied her hair back with a pink scarf and went out to the shed to fetch her bicycle.

"I'm just going for a ride," she said.

Her nonchalance was not lost on Mrs. Hollis. "Bit hot, isn't it?"

But Ruth had gone.

It was eight miles across country lanes to Fiddler's End, far enough for Ruth to have terrible pangs of doubt about what she was doing.

"But it can't be worse," she said to herself firmly, "than not knowing whether he bothers or whether he doesn't. If he chucks me out, I can forget him." She wouldn't, but she could start trying. She knew very well that there was much to be said for showing a boy one didn't care, and going out with somebody else, but she was too desperately honest to contemplate such a course. Since Gordon Hargreaves had found out that she had gone out with the same boy two

Saturdays running he had kept calling, turning his new car around in their narrow drive with a great deal of swanky revving, and suggesting a "run out," but Ruth could hardly bear to be civil to him. Peter McNair came down from the stables in his father's car to tell her that Toad was doing very well, and he looked at her as if he had heard the news, with a reflective light in his normally brotherly eye which she had never seen before, and asked her if she'd fancy going to see a film. But Ruth had laughed, and he hadn't minded a bit.

"I'm doing all the wrong things," she told herself, pedaling hard. But nothing would have turned her back. Her only panic was that it was too hot to work, surely? He would be somewhere else, gone swimming, or at home, and she wouldn't find him. Her sweaty pilgrimage would be in vain.

"Oh no!" she said out loud to the green elm-tops over her head, and they nodded at her passing, impassive, untroubled by her little human passion. "I love him," she said out loud again, and a passing car hooted at her and she shouted back, "Hog!"

The village hall at Fiddler's End had been built by the villagers themselves in 1929, and looked it. Ruth, approaching, saw that it was surrounded by empty prams, and realized that she had chosen clinic day. But the sight was comforting rather than disappointing, for it was the awful, actual moment of Pat's turning around and seeing her in the empty hall that she had dreaded most, and now, with lots of mothers and babies to blur the confrontation, she did not feel quite so frightened.

Not quite. It was still bad enough. She laid her bike against the wall and stood outside the door, her heart thudding. He was there, because she could hear the piano. The sound petrified her. She could not bring herself to open the door.

Someone else opened it from the inside and a child walked into her knees.

"Oh, Trevor, look where you're going!" said its mother.

Ruth disentangled herself, smiled like an idiot, and went in, because the woman was holding the door. She felt almost faint, and leaned against the wall, telling herself it was the eight miles, not Pat. But she knew it was Pat. She could not take another step.

The piano was on the stage, along with a pile of rickety cardtables, sagging screens, and ancient wooden folding chairs. Pat had his back to her, and was playing what sounded like some sort of a scale. He had on a faded blue shirt, pulled out over his jeans, the sleeves rolled up. His eyes on the music in front of him, he seemed oblivious of several toddlers who were climbing on to the stage and jumping off with shouts of glee right behind him, the whistling of a boiling kettle somewhere in the wings and the general hubbub of about thirty babies, half of them crying, and thirty mothers, most of them talking, several helpers in white coats giving orders and a group of tea-makers putting out cups and saucers. Ruth stared, her mental image of lonely genius at work shattered.

A woman in a white coat bustled up to her and said, "Look, dear, just go and tell the doctor I've got the umbilical hernia waiting, if he doesn't mind. It's very crotchety in this heat and its mother wants to get home. He's through the door at the bottom."

Ruth went, knocked at the door and put her head in. A doctor was poised over a baby, who was screwing up its face ready to yell. He looked up, and the baby, reprieved, paused in its intake of angry breath. Ruth got her message in quickly, and the doctor said, "Very well. Tell her I'm through with this now. I'll have it next."

Ruth took the news back to the nurse.

"Take him a cup of tea, dear," she said. "Go and tell the ladies. They forget him if I don't watch. No sugar."

Ruth went over to the tea-urn, and said, "Can I have one for the doctor?"

"Oh, yes. Give him the cup with the roses on, Maud. It isn't cracked. He doesn't take sugar. Here you are, dear."

Ruth took it. The doctor said, "Marvellous. Tell nurse there's a box of cotton-wool in the back of my car, will you? I shall want it before I'm through. Here's the key."

Ruth took the message back and the nurse said, "It's the red Cortina, dear, round the back. Thank you ever so much."

Ruth fetched the cotton-wool and delivered it and heard one of the tea-ladies shrill down the hall, "Do you want a cup of tea, Pat? How many sugars?"

"Two," he called back.

Ruth went back to the tea-urn and said firmly, "I'll take it."

"Oh, thank you, dear. I'll stir it first. We're short of spoons."

Ruth took the cup of tea down the hall, her hands shaking a little bit. She climbed up on to the platform and put it on the top of the piano.

"Your tea."

"Thanks," Pat said. He did not stop playing, or even look up. Ruth did not move, watching his hands doing something extraordinarily complex, and the back of his head, the neck slightly bent, the hair looking damp with the heat. And as she didn't go away, he looked up and, although he did not stop playing, he hit two wrong notes which even Ruth recognized. She tried desperately to divine his reaction, not expecting—from him—anything as extreme as joy, but dreading a veiled exasperation. And in her anxiety she saw both: his eyes widen with what was surely pleasure, only to be immediately tempered by . . . she was not sure. Doubt, possibly. A withdrawal. But even then he smiled, still playing.

"You made me play two wrong notes," he said, and stopped. "That's very bad."

"Of me?" she asked hesitantly.

"No, of me."

"You don't mind?" she said. "It was so hot, I thought you might—well, it's too hot to play, I thought . . . I just missed you at lunchtime . . ."

"Cripes, yes, it is hot." He shoved his chair back and leaned backwards, making it creak dangerously.

"I thought you might be swimming or something. But I hadn't anything to do."

"The tide's high at six. I might go then." He took a watch out of his back pocket and looked at it. "I've only been going an hour." He looked at her reflectively, and she saw beads of sweat on his upper lip, and the scar. She remembered the policeman, and pushed the memory away. She met his eyes, and neither of them looked away. Pat sighed. Ruth felt terrible, drowned by his displeasure.

"I'm sorry," she whispered.

"No," he said. "You've got it all wrong." He put up a hand and pushed his hair off his forehead with an irritated gesture. "It's what I've *got* to do," he said. "Not what I want."

"All the time?"

"Yes. Now. I've got to play in a concert. Until after the concert."

"When is the concert?"

"Three weeks tomorrow."

"It's very important?"

"Yes. It's not just me making a fool of myself on my own, but playing with an orchestra. That concerto we heard at the Festival Hall."

62

Ruth was awed. "You!"

"It doesn't just happen," he said. "It takes hours and hours for months. I've packed in the bread, as from tomorrow, to give myself more time."

"Oh, I'm sorry. I do see! I'm sorry I came. I didn't realize it was like that!"

"I'm not sorry you came," he said. "I just have to explain why I can't take you out or anything. It's not because——" He hesitated. "Oh, God, you distract me!"

Ruth did not say anything, her inside expanding with a glory that left no breath for words. She told herself that he used the word "distract" strictly in the sense of distraction from his work, not in the sense of going out of his mind like an Elizabethan poet, but it was enough. It was a perfect word, and described her own feelings for him utterly.

He glanced at the watch again.

"Look, give me till—say—half-past five. Then we'll go for a walk down the river. If the hall was free tonight I'd stop now and work tonight instead, but it's the Youth Club Fridays. Would that be okay by you? Would you mind hanging around?"

"No."

"All right." He smiled, and pulled his chair up to the piano again. "It's a date."

"I'll come back at half-past five."

Ruth went out of the hall, not seeing anything. There was a playing-field outside, and a clump of elm trees, and a man mowing the cricket-pitch with a tractor-mower. Ruth lay in the shade of the elms, and through the open windows of the hall she could hear Pat playing again. Every time the man mowing came down the field the noise of the mower drowned the piano, but when he moved away in the opposite direction she could hear Pat again. They were complementary, the two aural evidences of man's hard work, ebbing and flowing, and Ruth lay curled, feeling the sun on her back and the coolness of the shade just covering her head, and basked in the sensation of being utterly, fantastically content. Even just lying there, smelling the new-mown grass and listening to the work and the fretful babies, she was aware of her privilege, even apart from the other incredible and magical knowledge that she had just received from Pat's very own lips: it was happiness strong enough to hurt. "Being me," she thought . . . "I would not be anyone, anyone, *anyone* else in the whole of the world, in the whole of outer space right to the farthest, farthest invisible star." And the music came down the keyboard like a waterfall finding its way over tumbled rocks, and the mower approached inexorably, throwing up its fountains of cropped green, spreading its aura of summer on the lightest of July zephyrs. Ruth turned on to her back and thought, "It is impossible to be happier than this. If only you could bottle it, like plums, for afterwards . . ." And the time was suspended, and everything was rolled into this exquisite essence of perfect content, until the prams started to move away and the noisy toddlers were guided to their teas, and the doctor came out and slammed the doors of his red Cortina, and the sun had taken on the richness of late afternoon, the heaviness of its warmth hinting of over-ripeness, like a Mediterranean peach. Ruth felt herself sticky and lax with the heat. The mowing man finished. Ruth asked him the time, and he said, "Quarter to five."

She had the piano all to herself. It was playing the same thing over and over again, very deliberately. Some little boys came and started playing with the drinking fountain, squirting it in all directions. Two of them went over to the hall and hung through the open windows, shouting, "Pat, play us 'Instant Love'!" But the music did not falter in its stride.

At twenty past five, Ruth went into the hall again and sat

on one of the rickety chairs by the door. She thought she would make no noise at all, but the ancient chair betrayed her with its complaint. Pat turned around and she said hastily, "I'm ten minutes early. Don't stop!"

"It's all right, I'm through," he said.

She went over to the platform and stepped up beside the piano. "I've been listening, outside. Lying in the sun."

"Poor you! Did it send you to sleep?"

"No." She hesitated. He was closing the lid. "Will you play me something? Before we go. Just short."

" 'Red Sails in the Sunset'?" He grinned.

"No."

He opened the lid again. "The scale of C major?"

"No."

He considered for a moment, then started to play a piece that was very familiar to Ruth, although she had no idea what it was. It was lilting and wistful, and she could have sung the melody if she had wished.

"All right?" He raised his eyebrows inquiringly.

"Yes. Exactly."

It was effortless and perfect, and he played it through to the end, closing with the softest and most delicate chords, which hung and faded in the quiet hall like the grains of dust raining through the evening sunlight. Ruth was touched. It was all that she had wanted. He did not move until there was complete silence again, then he closed the lid without saying anything, and stood up, shoving back the chair. He looked moved too, but to gloom, Ruth thought, with a touch of anxiety.

"We'll go." He jumped down from the platform, and she followed. They went out of the door into the heat, and he locked it behind him.

"What was that piece?"

"A Brahms waltz."

"Hasn't it got a name?" She wanted it to remember.

"Number fifteen. Opus thirty-nine."

It hadn't sounded like numbers, to Ruth. She walked by his side, and he changed again, the gloom dispersing.

"We'll go down the river, and afterwards you can come back and have tea. Mrs. Bates won't mind."

The village street was short; a few cottages and council houses, a post-office, a grocer's, and a church, and a lot of elm trees petered out in a gravel lane with high hedges on either side. Midges swarmed and bit in the shade, and skylarks rose up from the grass behind the hedge, shrilling and hovering.

"It's a dead-end, this place," Pat said. "Doesn't go anywhere. Nothing happens."

"It's your home? You've always lived here?"

"Yes. I was born here."

"I like these sort of places."

"It's all right, compared with some. Change from London, anyway."

The lane opened out, giving on to pastures and a sea-wall, with some boatsheds and boats pulled out. When they climbed the wall, the river was at their feet, lipping over half-submerged acres of sea-lavender, shining and tranquil in the fullness of the tide. A few boats swung at moorings, quiet as swans. A man came out of the boatshed and said, "Hullo, Pat." He looked at Ruth as if considering the lines of a boat.

"Hi, Jim," Pat said.

He turned and led the way along the sea-wall, away from the boatshed. There was nothing, only the flatness of re-claimed pasture, and the line of the wall, curving, with withies to mark the mud, and the swamps of sea-lavender bathing in the tide. The sky was cloudless, the skylarks invisible, only the shrillness falling. Pat flung himself down

66

in the long grass where the wall changed direction and the sun beat straight across on to the slope.

"Fiddler's End Riviera," he said. "Welcome."

He shut his eyes, stretched out on his back, his hands clasped behind his head. Ruth slipped down beside him, rested her chin on her knees, and looked out over the water. "It's better than Northend," she said. "Why do they go there?"

"To leave this for us," Pat said. He turned his head and looked at her, squinting against the sun. "I'm going to swim. I suppose you're too well brought-up to swim in your underwear?"

"Yes. Besides, I can't. I'd drown." The warnings her mother had given her swam into her head as she watched Pat undress, and drowned too. He was all prepared, with swimming-trunks on under his jeans.

"There's no bath at Bates'," he said. "We have to make the best of days like this."

He flung his clothes up on the wall and stretched his legs out down the slope into the water. He had long straight toes to match his fingers, and brown hairy legs. Ruth remembered Gordon Hargreaves' girlish white legs at the Northend Lido, and giggled. Round his neck Pat wore a gold chain with a small medallion hanging on it. It was old and worn, like a rubbed coin, with what looked like a man's head in relief. Ruth was curious, wondering whether any sentimental associations were attached. The thought disturbed her.

Pat flicked some water at her.

"Go on," Ruth said. "Chicken!"

"I'll take you with me if you don't watch out."

He got up and waded out across a narrow stretch of salting to where a line of stakes showed where the steep bank was, groped for a moment for a foothold hidden under the

67

surface, and dived in. Ruth pulled his discarded shirt towards her, and lay back, using it to keep the scratchy grass off her neck and face. She watched Pat swim away against the tide, not taking her eyes off him, until it was hard to see him against the brilliance of the sun on the water. He swam like he played the piano, not just an idle dabble, but properly, like the life-savers on Northend beach. She had known it would be like that; she had known that he would not let her down: that he would not be flabby and white and feeble. Nothing he could do now would be wrong in her eyes. She was perfectly safe.

About fifteen minutes later he came back and lay on his front in the grass beside her to dry.

"Better than work," he said, and sighed.

"You're a very good swimmer."

"Yeah. I'm good at useless things. Swimming and soccer and playing the piano. Where do they get you?"

"The piano's getting you somewhere surely?"

"It's such ruddy hard work. And how do I know if anything'll come of it?"

"What about this concert then? Someone must think you're good enough. Won't all the critics come, and shout bravo, and give you rave notices? And you'll be famous overnight?"

"No. The critics will write, 'As yet his technique lacks the reserves required by an aspiring virtuoso in this demanding part.' And you know they can't play a flaming scale themselves. And all the fat aldermen of Northend will come to see if I'm worth my grant."

"It's going to be in Northend then?"

"Yes. At the Pavilion."

"Is it to do with this German exchange, with the town Northend is twinned with, or whatever they call it? 'A cultural exchange' . . . I've read about it in the paper."

"Yes. That's it. We've sent them a load of hammy song-and-dancers off the end of the pier, and they're sending us one of the best orchestras in Europe. It's stopping off here on its way to America. And our egg-headed town council thought it would be nice to have a local boy as soloist. And if I don't feel like it, they might not feel like continuing my grant."

"Is that what they said?"

"It's what they meant. They wrapped it up with a lot of hot air."

"What did they say about it at college? Your Professor?"

"Oh, he thinks it's the chance of a lifetime."

Ruth picked a blade of grass. "I see why you have to work. I didn't know all this." The whole idea of what he was up against was very sobering. She imagined most music students had cultured backgrounds with encouraging parents, not Mrs. Bates with no bathroom. She felt sure Clarissa had a bathroom.

"Can I come to the concert?"

"If you want. They've graciously given me six free tickets. You can have them all."

She turned her head and considered him, concerned and frowning. He turned at the same time and pressed down the grass that blurred his view of her face, and looked at her in the same way the man outside the boatshed had looked at her.

"Are you sure you won't come for a swim?"

She shook her head, aware now that he had good reason to think her an easy girl, since she had cycled eight miles without an invitation merely to see him. A cold doubt squeezed her, and her mother's words, nebulous as the rising heat that quivered over the horizon, touched her and were forgotten. She thought she knew everything, and she knew that she knew nothing. She knew that she ought to get up and start walking back, but she just went on sitting there, watching how the water ran off his hair and in sliding, hesitant drops down over the muscles of his back. He didn't say any more, but laid his cheek on his hand and shut his eyes. His face was cold and angry.

"Why did you come?" he said. "It doesn't help anything at all."

Ruth felt sick. She got up and stood for a moment, breaking a stalk of grass over and over in her hand.

"It's not all me . . . you asked me before . . ." But there wasn't anything to say that would put the moment right. The river and the setting sun were still so lovely that it hurt. She started walking back along the sea-wall, the heat striking her back, the midges in a cloud around her head. The tide had turned and the sea-lavender was uncovering in hazy blue profusion to meet the mud. Ruth felt nothing. She came to the boatshed and the man who had said hullo was just locking up. He had secured the padlock, and came to the top of the wall where the steps were just as Ruth arrived at the same spot. It was necessary to say something and he said, "After you."

"Thank you."

She went down the steps and he followed her.

"What've you done with Pat?" he said.

She shook her head, not trusting herself to say anything, and the man said, "Tch, tch, tch," with his tongue against his teeth. He fetched a bicycle that leaned against a store of timber, and put his leg over the saddle.

"He's a funny lad," he said. "Always was."

He cycled away. Ruth supposed she should follow, and find her own bicycle, but she had no will to walk any farther. She told herself it was the heat, and sat on the pile of timber, looking back the way she had come. She remembered earlier and the feelings she had wanted to bottle for future use. She had not thought she would need it so soon. The fall from such heights was like being hanged, breaking one's neck. "Dramatizing!" she mocked at herself. It happened all the time; the incident was described by a simple, paltry little word: tiff. Like sniff and piffle. Infinitesimal. She picked at a splinter of wood, pulling a long string out of the grain, hurting her finger-nails.

In the distance, Pat got up and pulled on his jeans and shirt. He started walking back along the sea-wall, hands in pockets, staring at the ground, kicking the grass. Ruth pulled at another splinter. He must have seen her, pink against the store-shed, but he took no avoiding action, and Ruth went on sitting there, the blood thudding. He came down the steps and looked at her, his face still dark.

"Come on. Let's go and get some tea."

Ruth slipped off the timber and they walked up the lane. Everything seemed much more real to Ruth this time, than when they had walked down. She was suspended, her feelings put away. Pat did not say anything at all, until they had walked through the village and came to the gate of the end cottage, a nineteen-twenties semi-detached with a privet hedge in front.

"This is Bates," He pushed open the gate and waited for her.

"I'll go home," she said. "It doesn't matter."

"No. She won't mind. Come on."

Ruth went up the path and Pat followed. "Go on in," he said.

The kitchen door was open and a fat grey-haired woman was buttering bread at a table. She was comfortable and motherly-looking in a way Ruth thought of as old-fashioned.

"My, it's hot," she said. "Come through, dear. I know I take up a lot of room, but you're little enough."

"This is Ruth," Pat said.

"Pleased to meet you, dear."

"I said she could stay to tea."

"All right, dear. It's just salad, but there's plenty of ham and tomatoes. I've laid the table in the other room. It won't be a minute. Take her through, Pat."

Ruth thought, in spite of her easy way, her eyes didn't miss much, taking her in, and resting reflectively on Pat's closed-up face. She was shrewd, as well as pleasant in her manner.

"Can I take something?" Ruth asked her.

"Yes, the tomatoes. And the sugar. There you are. The kettle's on already. It won't be a minute. You look as if you could do with a cup of tea."

"Yes. Thank you. I could."

Ruth took the things and went through into the other room, which was very small, with French windows opening on to a strip of garden. The table was covered with a chenille cloth, and a white damask one, and there was a vase of plastic roses pushed against the wall. There were two fireside chairs in green moquette and a tiled fire-place with photographs on the mantelpiece, and a television set. Pat turned on the television and sat down in the chair facing it. Ruth put down the tomatoes and the sugar and went back for more. It was almost as if Pat wasn't there at all, but she felt strangely at home.

"There's just the two of you, dear. Dad'll be late tonight. There's a darts' match and they're going in the coach. Here's the tea. I think that's everything. I'll just do a spot of ironing and leave you in peace. Shout if you want anything."

"Yes. Thank you. That's lovely."

She went back with the tea. There was soccer on the television and Pat came to the table watching it, and sat with his back to the window where he could see it.

"I thought soccer was a winter thing," Ruth said.

Pat grunted. He reached for the tomatoes, and Ruth poured him a cup of tea and pushed it over. "It's just as if we're married," she thought, "me with the teapot and him with the telly and nothing to say."

"Thanks," he said. Ruth felt she had scored a point.

She did not venture anything else, but ate in silence. Pat ate and watched the television. When she had finished, Ruth got up and took her cup of tea and sat on the step of the French windows, looking down the garden. It was so stupid, she thought. But the way things happened. And afterwards you knew you should have said this or that, or made just one gesture, and it would have been all right. But now there wasn't anything that presented itself. The whole day was a horrible failure, and then afterwards, when she would start thinking about it, she could not bear to contemplate.

There was a sound of voices in the kitchen, Mrs. Bates' and a man's. The man's was loud and impatient, although Ruth could not catch the words. The kitchen door was around the corner from where she sat.

"Pat!" Mrs. Bates' voice called. "It's your father."

"What's he want?" Pat shouted back, still watching the screen.

"He wants you to help him move a wardrobe."

"Oh, go to hell," Pat said. Raising his voice he shouted, "I'm not going to lift things, you know that!" But he got up, all the same, and went to the door. "I won't be long," he said to Ruth, and went out. Ruth nearly said, "It won't make any difference," but didn't. She heard him go out through the kitchen, and his father's voice, and then the two voices receded down the garden path.

Mrs. Bates came in. "All right, dear?"

"Yes, thank you."

"Sorry about that. I told him Pat had someone with him, but you can't tell him anything, I'm afraid. He's like that. Whatever he wants, that's it."

Ruth was wondering whether she should go. She got up and put her cup and saucer on the table.

"Perhaps I ought to be getting along. I've got quite a way to go."

"Oh, you can't go before Pat comes back, dear!"

"I don't think he'll be much bothered," she said. She meant it to sound light, but it sounded bitter and shaky, the way she felt. She regretted it instantly.

"Pat's a very moody boy. Don't be upset," Mrs. Bates said. She looked at Ruth anxiously. "Here, have another cup of tea." She started pouring one out, before Ruth could say anything. "He could do with a nice girl like you. He works too hard."

"I don't think he wants to be—distracted."

"That's a matter of opinion. You stay with him, lovey. You're the sort. The one he had last year did him no good at all—a right nasty piece she was. And when they split up I was glad, I can tell you. But you're different. I can see you're a nice girl. Just what he needs."

"Interfering old busybody," Ruth thought. But the woman was kindly, and obviously spoke with concern for Pat, which warmed Ruth to her.

"That's my boy, on the mantelpiece." Mrs. Bates waved her hand to a photograph of a bearded young man with long hair. "He looks better without all that face fungus, but that's the way it is these days. He's a folk-singer. Done very well for himself. Funny, isn't it, the things they make a living at these days? There's the dad, worked on the farm all his life since he was fourteen, and not a penny saved, and there's John traveling all over the country, his own car, name in the *Radio Times* . . . makes me wonder sometimes."

74

"He must be good, to have got on like that. There's lots of competition."

"Yes, he always had a nice voice. Can't say as I like the stuff he sings though."

"He and Pat were at school together?"

"Yes. Pat lived over the road, but he was always in here. He set John off really—John was always very shy, and he wouldn't sing in public, but Pat used to bully him something terrible. He played the harmonica with him, it really did sound very nice. But there were times I used to worry —I used to think Pat was a bad influence on our boy. John's very quiet, you see. And Pat was—well—he got into a lot of trouble, put it that way. Pranks really, but he was wild compared with John. His parents were no help to him, that was at the bottom of it. The only good thing his mother ever did for him was make him keep on with his music. She used to nag him something awful. We used to think it funny, really, a rough lad like that, but it turned out she was right after all. It's amazing how well he's got on. Did he tell you about the concert he's playing in next month?"

Ruth nodded.

"I know he's played in lots of concerts before, but this one is a bit special—to us anyway. Being as it's in Northend and the mayor and the corporation and all that will be there, and this orchestra's very famous, I believe. We're all going—not as we care much for that sort of thing as a rule, but when it's in the family, so to speak . . ."

Ruth drank her third cup of tea, aware of a pang of regret for the uncomplicated baker's boy she had first set eyes on. Or was it sensing the complications that had been the attraction in the first place? If Pat had been a carefree roundsman, chatting her up and happy to stop for cups of tea in the kitchen, she would probably have been bored by him. The way it had turned out, she knew that a good part of Pat's attraction to her was this difficult core so amply explained by Mrs. Bates. She had always been attracted by difficulties. Both her ponies had been difficult, not ready-schooled, well-mannered animals like Gordon Hargreaves, but prickly, uncertain creatures with wild pasts . . . it all fitted in . . . she had only herself to blame.

She put the teacup on the table. "I really must go." The sun had gone, and she had no lights on her bike. "It's been very kind of you——"

"Oh, dear, you must see Pat before you're off. He's only across the road—go and shout him good-bye, dear. It's a bit awkward, you know—they don't like his preferring it here. Only natural, I suppose, but they can be nasty when they choose."

"I'm all right," Ruth said firmly. "I'll go and fetch my bicycle from the village hall, and I'll probably see him on my way back. Thank you very much for the tea."

She left as firmly as she had spoken, feeling stifled by all the currents that had flowed over her afternoon happiness. She wanted cool air and her own company, and the comfort of a few private tears. She fetched her bicycle, and got on it, and was coming back past the Bates' house when Pat came down the path of the house opposite. She saw him, wobbled, and called out, "Good-bye. I've got to go—I've got no lights."

"Hey, wait a minute!" he shouted.

She knew she should have kept on going, but she didn't. She stopped with one foot on the curb, and he came across the road.

"You've got time yet," he said.

"I'm going."

"I'll walk up to the main road with you."

She got off and started to push the bike, and he walked beside her. She wasn't going to say anything, but leave it to him, but he didn't say anything either, and they walked

76

in silence. When they got to the main road she got on again, angry and miserable.

"Good-bye then."

"Look, I——" He paused, looked at her, and looked away. "Oh, blast! It's no good. Leave it. Forget it. I'm sorry if I messed anything up for you."

And he turned and walked back the way he had come. Ruth shoved off from the grass verge, and set off for home.

Chapter Five

✸

"Well, I'm glad, and won't pretend otherwise," her mother said. "Don't expect me to. All the piano playing in the world doesn't alter the fact that he's got a very dubious past. I've heard that he's recently done time for 'causing grievous bodily harm.' I was going to ask you about it. Has he told you anything about it?"

"No!"

"Did you know?"

"No! I heard something—Maxwell said something, but not what it was for . . . I didn't ask."

"You don't want to know, do you?"

"No!"

"Oh, Ruth, see sense! You're well out of it."

"You think I can just switch it off! Like—like knocking off potatoes because you're slimming or something! He's not like anybody else!"

"It's only a crush. You'll go through it lots of times before you're married." The complacency of the remark goaded Ruth more than anything else her mother could have chosen to say.

"All right, you tell *me* how I feel! You don't know anything about it! You never did, else how could you say a thing like that? The way you—you and daddy—you've forgotten—forgotten what it's all about——"

She gave a great hiccup, the tears spurting up.

"Oh, Ruth," her mother said. "You just don't know." She

wasn't angry. Ruth picked up her empty teacup and flung it with all her force across the kitchen. It hit the wall above the kitchen door, just as Ted appeared in the doorway.

"Ruth!" Her mother sprang up, furious.

"Hey! It's just like home!" Ted said. "I come here for a bit of peace and quiet——"

"If I was Barbara I'd throw things at you too," Ruth shouted. "Always running back to mummy! You're all horrible!"

"Get out!" her mother said. "Go up to your room."

Ruth flounced around and slammed the door behind her.

"Good heavens!" Ted said. "What's up with her?"

"It's her love life," Mrs. Hollis said tightly, filling the kettle.

"Obviously not running smooth. It must be true."

"She thinks it's never happened to anyone else. She's so naïve."

"Everybody thinks nobody's ever suffered like they have. The only thing with me is, I don't just think, I know." He slumped down in the chair Ruth had so recently leaped out of. "Do you think there was some truth in what she said?"

"Probably. Oh, my children! Why are they so much more trouble than everyone else's——!"

"It's their upbringing," Ted said. "Don't you start suffering too. Let's all throw cups. It must relieve something."

"She's never done anything like that before. We've had ten days of utter misery, but no violence up till now."

"He's thrown her over, I take it?"

"Yes, but I don't know what happened exactly. I never asked her. What sparked this little incident off was my telling her I was pleased."

"The soul of tact."

"But he's done time, Ted! For assault. 'Grievous bodily

79

harm,' or whatever they call it. I mean, I think I'm very tolerant, but it would be a funny mother who approved of that."

"I wouldn't like to tangle with him. I thought that the first time I set eyes on him. She does choose 'em, doesn't she?"

"Well, when there's Gordon, and Peter . . . I know this one's got a very romantic profession, but——"

"Yes, but she fell for him when she thought he was just a baker's roundsman. It's the old black magic, Ma, you can't deny it. You don't understand——"

"Oh, don't you start!"

The kettle started to boil, and she turned to it automatically. At the same time there was a knock on the open door and someone said, "Is Ruth around?"

Ted, turning around abruptly, had the grace to blush. Mrs. Hollis thumped the teapot down with a crash that nearly sent it the same way as Ruth's cup, and said grimly, "Very much so."

"Come in," Ted said.

Pat stepped over the threshold and said, "I'd like to have a word with her." He looked neither embarrassed nor particularly friendly, but much as if he had come for the bread money.

"I thought——" Mrs. Hollis said, annoyed. Then she stopped herself, and poured the water into the teapot. "It's none of my business, I suppose. Call her, Ted."

Ted opened the door and roared up the stairs, "Ruth, Pat's here! He wants a word with you!"

There was a long silence, and then, distantly, "If you think that's funny——"

"Oh, heavens," Ted said, and went out, shutting the door behind him.

Mrs. Hollis got out the teacups, including one for Pat,

and the teaspoons and the sugar and the milk, all with great concentration. She could think of nothing to say to him, and he obviously wasn't going to volunteer a word. He stood leaning against the door-post, gazing into space, his hands in his pockets. He was wearing the usual jeans and a navy-blue tee-shirt, and the ominous physique was only too apparent. The words "grievous bodily harm" went through Mrs. Hollis's head again, the quaintness of the phrase accentuating its essential gravity, rather than adding any touch of charm. The coldness of his face did not invite her to question him. She lacked the required insolence, she told herself, and decided that the whole problem was man's work. If the friendship was on again, Ruth's father would have to have a chat with the boy. She poured the tea.

"You'll have one?"

"Thanks."

Gordon Hargreaves would have said, "Thank you very much, Mrs. Hollis. It's very kind of you."

Ted came in, grinning all over his face, and said, "She's on her way. Which is mine?"

"That one's got one sugar. How many do you have, Pat?"

"Two."

He moved off the door-post and came to the table. Ted kicked out a chair for him, and he sat down.

"You packed in the bread then?"

"Yeah. I had enough."

"You're not working now?"

"No. I'll get something else in a week or two. You can get jobs easy in Northend this time of year."

The door opened and Ruth came in. Pat turned and looked at her, and said, "Hullo."

She nodded at him, her white face flushing up. She took the cup of tea her mother passed to her, and carried it to the draining-board, and looked out across the garden. Mrs.

Hollis approved her nonchalance, but knew her well enough to realize that she did not trust showing her face to the room.

"I just came to see if you wanted to come up to London on Saturday. Make it a day," Pat said, equally nonchalant.

"What to do?"

"I've got to play in a concert. But afterwards I thought we could come back and meet Maxwell and his girl and have a meal and go to a disco or something. Whatever you'd like."

Ruth went on contemplating the garden, trying to stop the glory showing in her face.

"Yes, I don't mind."

"Where's the concert?" Mrs. Hollis asked. "The Festival Hall?"

Pat smiled faintly: "Not yet. This one's Hampstead. Somebody's church restoration fund."

The word Hampstead stung Ruth like a hypodermic needle. She turned around and looked keenly at Pat, but he showed neither cunning nor embarrassment. She opened her mouth to inquire further, but he smiled at her, and he was brown with swimming and his hair had grown and curled over his ears and she was lost. She felt herself plummeting, helpless.

"Yes," she said.

"It sounds frightfully respectable," Ted said.

"Yes, it is."

"And you'll bring her home, I take it, after the disco?" Mrs. Hollis put in. Ruth glared at her.

"Yes," Pat said.

He got up, and said to Ruth, "I'll meet you on the train, like we did before. Okay? Ten-forty from Northend."

"Yes. All right."

He moved over to the door. Ruth made to follow him but

her mother said, "Wash up the cups, Ruth. Come along. I've got to start getting a meal together and I want the table." She fixed Ruth with an eye that was impossible to ignore. Ruth glowered at her again. Pat went out and down the drive and Mrs. Hollis said sharply, "You don't have to show you're be*sotted*! Yes, yes, yes . . . I don't know!"

"No," said Ruth.

She was in a dream, and broke a cup.

"Any more today?" Mrs. Hollis asked, her voice edgy with despair.

"What did you say?" Ruth asked.

They met on the train, according to plan. Ruth, having considered the implications of the invitation very carefully since it was offered, had a good many suspicions in the back of her mind but resolved to say nothing. She did not want to nag. Nor did she want the worst of the suspicions confirmed. She would please her mother and not be besotted, and live in hopes that the day would turn out all right. She had dressed very carefully in a slightly hippyish dress of a peculiar reddish-brownish-purplish design which she considered suited her dark coloring and was the best she could muster against Clarissa. Her mother had groaned when she saw it, but Pat raised his eyebrows and said, "That's nice." Ruth felt herself purring inside. Pat had had a slight hair-cut, but otherwise looked as casual as usual; he had a tatty suitcase with his "other gear" in it.

The strongest of Ruth's suspicions was that Clarissa was the "right nasty piece" who had done Pat no good at all, according to Mrs. Bates. She had no real evidence for this, apart from the veiled, mutual bitterness that she had witnessed the day at the Festival Hall. She also had a very strong feeling that Pat was taking her merely to show her off to Clarissa.

"You're playing in this concert with Clarissa?" she asked him, just to get the basic facts straight.

He looked surprised. "Yes."

"I remember she said something about a Hampstead date when we met her at the Festival Hall."

"Oh, did she? I don't remember."

"You're playing a duet with her?"

"A Beethoven violin sonata."

"Violin?"

"She plays the violin. I play the piano."

"Oh." Ruth blushed, knowing that Pat knew she had thought he played the violin as well. Her ignorance was abysmal.

"Why are we going so early?"

"We've got to go to her house and run through it once or twice beforehand. The concert's at three. We won't have all that much time."

"Oh." So that was made clear. Ruth considered Pat, and decided that that was as much as she wanted to know, for the time being, on that precise subject.

"Don't you feel nervous," she asked, "playing in a concert?"

"Yes. Generally."

She was almost surprised that he admitted this.

"I won't be sorry when next Saturday's over," he said.

"When are you going to rehearse for that?"

"The Saturday morning, as far as I know."

"Is that all?"

"Yes. With them, that is. They aren't due to arrive till Friday night."

Ruth remembered her feelings, considering the lonely pianist at the Festival Hall, and the burden of his responsibility. Pat surprised her by saying, "It's only the same as this show-jumping thing. You practice, and hope for the best when the time comes. Don't you ever feel nervous?"

"But it's not the same! If I make a mistake, it's part of the fun for the spectators. But if you make a mistake——"

"If I thought I was going to make a mistake, I wouldn't be there," Pat said. "But I can do it well or do it badly—afterwards I know, the same as you."

"I suppose so. Even if you don't exactly have a score."

She considered him again.

"You look very tidy with your hair cut."

"That's for the Prof. He says if you look like a student they'll think you play like a student."

"Will he be there?"

"I shouldn't think so."

"Will he be there next Saturday?"

"Yes." He groped around in his back pocket and brought out some tickets. "These are what they gave me. Did you want one?"

"Can I have more than one? My mother would like it, and my father. We'll pay for them." It would be a marvellous opportunity, she thought, to show Pat off to her parents at his best. She was sure they would come, out of curiosity.

"No, I don't want them. Here." He gave her six, then took one back. "I'd better keep one for Mrs. Bates."

"What about your parents?"

"They can buy theirs," he said.

"And the Prof?"

"Oh, he'll have his own. There'll be a few of them coming from London, I imagine. I'll be seeing him on Monday anyway. I'm going up to work with him next week."

"In London?"

"Yes."

"You'll stay in town?"

"I expect so."

Ruth told herself there was no future in it. Not to expect

anything. He had his reasons for asking her today, and they were not her reasons for wanting to be with him. She looked out of the window, too frightened to look forward to anything, frightened for how much it mattered.

The journey to Hampstead was complicated. There was a tube, and a bus, and then they were walking down a quiet tree-lined street with gigantic mansions on either side with gravelled drives and opulent cars in waiting. Ruth felt a quiet horror stealing over her.

"Does Clarissa live down here?"

"Yes."

Her essentially conformist, narrow upbringing had never prepared Ruth for the extremes that Pat seemed to take in his stride: she was going to be as out of her depth here as in the Jolly Sailor on a Saturday night. She had nothing to flaunt at Clarissa, not her looks, her intelligence, or even Pat's regard. She was silent. The houses were the sort Prime Ministers lived in, she thought. Opposition Prime Ministers. Pat, apparently, had none of her diffidence; he turned in at Clarissa's drive as if he were delivering two large uncut. The house was all gabled windows and wisteria and an oak-studded door fit for a castle; a gardener was pruning roses, and a maid answered the door.

"Come in," she said.

They went in. Pat did not wait for the maid, but crossed the hall, an expanse of parquet and Persian carpets, and opened one of the doors that opened off it. Ruth scurried after him and Pat turned and said to the maid, "Tell her we've arrived, will you?"

"Yes, sir," the maid said.

"Golly, have you got a lot of friends like this?" Ruth asked, as Pat unceremoniously slammed the door behind them. They were in what was presumably the music room; it was white and gold, with French doors giving on to a lawn mown in velvet strips like an advertisement for fertilizer, and furnished with an enormous grand piano, several music-stands, and some Victorian button-backed chairs in gold velvet to match the curtains. Ruth leaned against the door, taking it in. She had only seen its like before in magazines. It was the epitome of gracious living, spoiled only by Pat in his jeans and jersey dropping his bag on the fitted carpet.

He grinned.

"Yeah, smart, isn't it? And what a piano! Only the tuner ever plays it, and the odd accompanist once in a blue moon." His face went serious and he added, "It doesn't make any difference. She doesn't play any the better for it."

The honest sense of his scale of values made Ruth ashamed.

"I'm such a snob," she said. "This sort of thing impresses me terribly."

"I used to think that. But it doesn't mean a thing in any way that matters. Only that it makes you jealous—this piano—nothing else . . ." He opened the piano and sat down and played some chords. "It's beautiful. I used to play here quite a lot. I've never played on a better piano than this one. It's an old one, a family heirloom . . ."

Ruth sat down in one of the velvet chairs, watching him, trying to reconcile the old jeans and the baker's round and the concert pianist. He had as many sides as an old three-penny bit, and as many moods to match. She could not follow him. And why did he used to play here quite a lot? Presumably before the three months in prison . . . ? She glowered at him, painfully trying to fathom the maze he was forever presenting. At least with dullness one knew where one was.

"You look good," he said from the piano.

She resisted, not smiling, resenting bitterly the emotions

he evoked in her, and did nothing to comfort. If he had had the mentality of Gordon Hargreaves he would have played her the Brahms waltz to woo her, but he only grinned in a mocking way, and started to play an intricate passage which she suspected was out of his concerto.

Clarissa came in. Ruth was satisfied to note the startled expression that overcame her composure when she saw her sitting in the chair.

"Oh!" She shot Pat a furious glance, which Ruth did not miss. Then she recovered herself and said with a fair amount of grace, "Hullo. Ruth, isn't it?"

"Yes. Hullo."

"She's going to turn the pages for me," Pat said.

Ruth felt her stomach give a jump of surprise.

Clarissa said coldly, "You turned the pages yourself the last time."

"Yes, well, I hadn't got Ruth to help me then."

Clarissa said, "While I remember, they asked me if you can play the Moonlight Sonata, because some pillar of the church has requested it, and they think she's good for fifty pounds if she's treated properly. I said yes."

"Very considerate of you."

"I've got the music if you want it. Have you got a copy of the 'Spring'? Or do you want mine?"

"I've brought my own." He went to his bag and opened it. Clarissa said, "If that's your suit in there, it ought to go on a hanger. Give it to me."

Pat took out the music and gave the bag to Clarissa, who went to the door and shouted for the maid. Ruth went over to the piano and said softly, anxiously, "I can't read music. You know I can't. Why did you say that?"

Pat sat down and pulled a chair up close to the stool.

"Sit down," he said.

Ruth hesitated. She felt angry, being forced into a role

she had no desire for. But Pat turned and smiled at her, very easy, and said, "There's nothing to it. I'll show you what to do. Sit down."

She sat down, angry because she was too feeble to remonstrate. Yes, yes, yes, as her mother had pointed out so scornfully. The chair was so close that her knee touched his thigh. She shifted it back. He smiled at her again. She felt lost and hopeless. She transferred her gaze to the music, which appalled her. Even the writing at the top was in a foreign language.

She knew nothing. Clarissa came back to the piano with her violin, her glance very cool. Pat gave her an A, and she started to tune her instrument.

"I'll tell you when," he said to Ruth. "And don't worry. I won't come to a full stop if you get hung up."

Ruth sat back, deciding to be as cool as Clarissa. Clarissa looked very noble, poised with her bow; Ruth could not help but be impressed. Pat pushed up his jersey sleeves and said, "Okay?" and Clarissa gave an imperial nod and launched forth with a bold, high note into a jaunty little tune, while Pat made a soft rippling accompaniment underneath. Very secondary for him, Ruth decided: how satisfactory for bossy Clarissa, keeping him in his place, but then Clarissa stopped, and the piano ran rapidly up from underneath and took the tune over, very gay and delicate, with Clarissa doing the donkey-work underneath. Ruth stared at the printed page, and supposed that the close-together notes making black slopes were the rapid scales; of the rest, the pencilled numbers and hieroglyphics that looked like the sign for pylons on an ordnance survey map, she could make nothing. But Pat, his fingers moving very fast, said, "Ruth, now," and she stood up and turned as neatly and delicately as befitted a third member of this gifted group. Pat played a very loud and decisive chord, and launched off alone over another very black and mountainous track. Clarissa waited for him, putting in her piece like a teasing wife, and then went skipping very frivolously over a lot of dark close-together notes for Pat until she came to a little questioning melody, which Pat repeated, so that the two instruments, it seemed to Ruth, were having a conversation. Ruth stopped being confused, and became fascinated instead, eavesdropping on the complex pattern of the argument. She realized, very dimly, that—whatever Pat might have said about doing it to pay for the mortgage—there was a good deal more to it than that. Pay for the mortgage it might, but it was not what either of them was thinking as they wove the intricate web of the sonata. There was an absorption and a *rapport* which Ruth could feel as she sat on the edge of her chair; it communicated, as if she were the whole audience of the supporters of the crumbling church, so that the dying, echoing tune at the end of the adagio, delicate and soft as a far-away pigeon's call, repeated on both the violin and the piano and dying with a last scarcely perceptible chord, had her moved almost to tears. The last murmur faded, Pat moved his hands off the keys and rested them on his knees. His expression was so distant, so tender, that Ruth scarcely knew him. There was a long, perfect silence, then he turned the page of the music and started to play the scherzo, which was as light and joky as a new-born lamb trying out its legs. Ruth had never thought it of Beethoven. She watched Clarissa watching Pat, and saw his eyes flick to hers, his hands waiting, and then they went racing up a long scale together, and Ruth found her place in the music again, and thought, "They've done it together lots of times before." It was something Clarissa had over her that she could not touch, this professional thing between them that was quite outside her experience. She concentrated on watching for the page-turning, seeing where Pat's eyes had got to. Once he swore and said something to Clarissa she did not catch, but without interrupting his playing; Ruth thought suddenly of the Jolly Sailor and the blonde woman saying, "Don't be long, darling," and she thought that Pat didn't have a pigeon-hole anywhere. She turned a page and found that there weren't any more to turn, and she relaxed and watched Pat, his stern profile and the underlip jutting slightly in the deep seriousness of his concentration.

When it was finished, he discussed several points with Clarissa and they went back and played different sections over again. Ruth found that she could pick up a few landmarks out of the maze, like "tr" for trills, which were recognizable even to her, and dots for staccato passages, and her page-turning improved, accomplished after a mere nod from Pat.

"We haven't forgotten much," Pat said to Clarissa. "It should sound all right."

"*I'm* happy," Clarissa said, putting her violin away. "Lunch will be ready, I should imagine. Do you want to come up to the bathroom, Ruth? I'll show you."

"Have you got the other music? The Moonlight?" Pat asked. "I'd like to go through it."

"It's in that cupboard."

Ruth followed Clarissa out of the room and up the curving, close-carpeted staircase. The bathroom was close-carpeted too, with enormous mirrors and gold rings for the towels, which each had a monogrammed C-S in the corner. Ruth tried not to be impressed; at least, not to show it. She washed her hands and Clarissa combed her gorgeous hair. Faintly downstairs the piano could be heard, the gentle air mingling in a soothing summer manner with the occasional snip of the gardener's pruning shears among the fading roses. The hot sun came through the wisteria leaves on to the white porcelain, and Ruth felt one of her familiar, strange longings for something quite out of her reach, out of her experience. With everything unresolved, not really happy, yet strangely content to be just so, with life's possibilities spread out this way and that way, Ruth was suspended in that little moment, with the smell of soap and roses and the sound of the piano.

"Is Pat good?" she asked Clarissa, wanting to know.

Clarissa pushed a towel back through the ring.

"Oh, yes. He's Professor Hampton's darling boy. In spite of everything."

Ruth looked at Clarissa steadily. "What do you mean? In spite of everything?"

Clarissa looked at her curiously, almost suspiciously. "Don't you know?" She shrugged. Downstairs in the hall a gong rang out and a feminine voice called out, "Clarissa!"

"Oh, it doesn't matter," Clarissa said. She opened the door and shouted, "Coming!"

A *Vogue*-like woman was waiting in the hall—for the fashion photographer, Ruth thought, rather than for lunch.

"This is my mother, Mrs. Cargill-Smith," Clarissa said. "Ruth."

"How do you do," said Mrs. Cargill-Smith, looking rather puzzled. "Do you play——?"

"She turns over," Clarissa said. "She's a friend of Pat's."

"Oh." Two very elegant eyebrows arched in surprise. Ruth, with a dart of perception, saw in Mrs. Cargill-Smith her own mother, trying to divine relationships, not wanting to ask, but avidly curious. It was just the same, in spite of the setting and the money. "It doesn't make any difference," Pat had said. "Oh, he is right!" Ruth thought. "He isn't taken in like me." Whatever did Mrs. Cargill-Smith think of Pat? she wondered, her eyes widening with a delicious curiosity, every bit as avid as that of Mrs. Cargill-Smith.

"Tell Pat it's waiting," the woman said to Clarissa. "So

you're a friend of Pat's," she added to Ruth, leading the way into the dining-room. "At the college?"

"No, at home."

"Really? You'll be at the concert next Saturday then?"

"Yes."

"What a splendid opportunity for him! He is so fantastically talented. We shall all feel so proud, seeing him play under Backhaus. Sit here, dear."

Ruth sat. The Cargill-Smith eyes, mother and daughter, had a devastating coldness, counting all the pros and cons, hawks over stubble. Ruth wanted desperately to know what had happened between Pat and Clarissa. He was perfectly at home in this house, coming in for lunch when the rest of them were half-way through and departing without waiting for coffee, and without apology. The conversation was of music, nothing of any personal interest at all, very safe ground, and Ruth saw Mrs. Cargill-Smith trying to draw conclusions, and failing. She was a conventionally smart and good-looking woman, but her features were hard and Ruth guessed that her perfect upper-class manner, hiding everything, hid a good deal of unpleasantness. Clarissa would be like that when she was forty. Ruth wondered if she would grow like her own mother when she was forty. She hoped not; she did not think she could ever become so insensitive and dull.

Ruth was bothered by whether she was doing the right things with all the cutlery, the bread rolls, the napkins and thanking the maid, but Pat obviously had no such qualms, reaching for what he wanted and scooping up some more potatoes without waiting to be asked. After the peach melba he pushed back his chair and got up.

"You haven't got to play that other thing," Clarissa said. "I didn't promise them anything. Not if you can't manage it."

She was not a gracious girl, Ruth thought, the way she spoke. There was an acidity, getting at Pat. It occurred to Ruth then, seeing Clarissa's expression suddenly as Pat moved towards the door, that the ungraciousness covered resentment, that Clarissa was not immune to Pat at all, for all her imperious manner. And Ruth knew that her guess as to why Pat had asked her to come along was perfectly correct: she was his armor, stopping any advance on Clarissa's part.

"I don't mind," Pat said, and went out.

They drank coffee and Ruth was questioned about her future plans and her school exams. The piano behind two closed doors raged furiously.

Mrs. Cargill-Smith looked at her watch and said, "Two o'clock. You'd better get changed, Clarissa. Tell Pat he can use the green bathroom. We ought to leave at half-past."

They got up from the table and went out into the hall.

"Whatever's he playing?" Ruth asked. "I thought——"

"The third movement," said Clarissa's mother. "The thunderclouds come up, you know. Nothing is pure moonlight all the way."

"Very philosophical," said Clarissa bitterly.

"Don't be silly, dear. Run along. I'll see to Pat. Perhaps you'd like to wait in the sitting-room, Ruth."

Ruth waited, having plenty to think about.

Ruth thought she would die, walking on to the stage behind Clarissa and Pat, across acres of polished parquet to the insular piano, taking her hard chair while they bowed. If she had known Pat was going to do this to her, she would never have come. Her hands were trembling. She clasped them tightly, and looked at Pat's, which were perfectly composed. She supposed he was nervous, but he didn't appear to be. He looked a complete stranger in a formal dark suit and tie, and Ruth had the feeling that she had wandered into an alien world: the unfamiliarity of both the situation and feelings unnerved her completely. And all the time there was this great uncertainty, that he was using her. Mrs. Cargill-Smith could have turned for him far more usefully than she could. She felt as far away from him as when she had left him the evening at Fiddler's Creek, and yet her knee was touching his piano stool. He had scarcely spoken a word since they had left the house, but now he turned to her, while Clarissa was tuning her violin, and said, "All right?"

"No," Ruth whispered, not letting him have it all his own way. "I'm distracted."

He gave her a startled glance, looking very much the old Pat, and Ruth was comforted by shaking him. It wasn't kind at such a moment, but nor was he. Clarissa turned, her bow lifted, and fixed him with her eye. He recovered himself immediately. Ruth saw his lower lip go out, very grim; he gave Clarissa a little nod, and they were away. Ruth turned in exemplary fashion, every crumpled corner gained like a triple-bar cleared without a fault. "Yes," she thought, softened by Beethoven running through her blood-stream, watching Pat's face moved by what he was doing, "I love you, I love you, you beast." He nodded and she got up and turned two pages at once, completely demoralizing herself, although Pat went on playing as if nothing had gone wrong. "He knows it," she thought. "He's got me here completely under false pretenses." And then it was the last page, and her reluctant part was over. The audience clapped and roared and bravoed, and Pat and Clarissa did very correct bows to the front and both sides while Ruth stood up, not knowing what to do at all. Pat, guessing her plight, turned around and said, "Follow me," and they made an exit in single file, Clarissa first. The dark openings of the wings of

95

the stage were like going to earth, private and quiet and blessed. When they got there Clarissa turned to Pat, looking white and ravaged, and said, "Oh, I'm glad it's over! I made a mess of the scherzo."

"It was all right," Pat said.

They went back again for two more bows; then when the audience had quieted down, Pat went back again alone to do the requested sonata, which Ruth was overwhelmingly relieved to see he was going to play without music. Clarissa disappeared but Ruth went on leaning against the wings, soothed by the moonlight and thinking of the remark, "Nothing is pure moonlight all the way." "Why not?" she wondered. "Why can't it be?" She looked at Pat, and he appeared to be looking back at her, although she knew he wasn't. She thought, "After today I shall know where I am with him. Whether it's finished or just starting." And then she remembered that she had thought that the last time. Perhaps she would never know, like Ted never really knew with Barbara, although he was married to her. "People," she thought, "are much more difficult than horses." And God knew, she had found them hard enough. But, like the moment in the bathroom, she was satisfied, watching Pat, lapped by the gentle melody and knowing that afterwards he was going to come to her and take her home. Not Clarissa. Clarissa would have to say good-bye, pretending she didn't care. Ruth felt a terrible pang for Clarissa. The music skipped into a very innocent, charming little tune, much gayer than the first movement, but Ruth kept hearing the warnings underneath, as if it was talking to her, telling her to watch out, a falling of low wistful notes from the skipping of the right hand. Getting ready for the thunderstorm. In her emotional state, overwrought from the page-turning, she thought of it as an omen. She shut her eyes, and the thunder came, a torrent of arpeggios, scaring all

the old ladies in the hall into startled attention. "Oh, God,"
Ruth prayed, "don't let it go wrong again. Let it be moonlight." She had an awful feeling that something terrible was
going to happen; it was a very clear and certain feeling,
and took all the strength out of her knees.

Pat came off, looking absent and hot, wiping his face
with a disreputable handkerchief that spoiled his professional image.

"What's the matter?" he said to her. "You look as if you've
seen a ghost."

She shook her head. The feeling had gone but she felt
drained, as if she had been doing all the work, not Pat. It
was the heat, she thought. The hall was very hot. Perhaps
the thunder was real. Pat had to go back twice more to
bow, and afterwards, while the church choir was forming
up on stage for the next item, he had to shake some rev-
erend hands back-stage, and be polite. But at last he came
to her and said, "Did you put my Spring Sonata back in
the bag?" and she nodded and he said, "Let's get the hell
out of here."

And they were out in the sunshine and the traffic, and
Ruth felt that it was going to be all right after all.

Chapter Six

✸

They went back to Liverpool Street and caught the train home. Ruth felt she had grown up during the day. She was not prepared to be a doormat anymore; she realized that her dog-like devotion was not enough, either for Pat or for herself; the relationship needed more nourishment, or it was going to die. And it was for Pat to decide. She thought he would. She felt cool, and optimistic, and about five years older than the day before. She didn't say anything at all. Pat didn't seem to notice, being in a cloud himself, but when they were on the train, and she had merely gazed out of the window for three stations, she became aware that he was conscious of the situation. He was watching her, and glowering slightly. Five stations later the man sitting next to Ruth got out, which left an old man asleep in the far corner, and Pat leaned forward and said, "Ruth."

Ruth looked at him.

He said, "I'm sorry if you didn't like it—if you thought ——" He hesitated. "It was work, you see. I didn't want it to be anything else. And with Clarissa it's very difficult now. But that engagement to play was arranged by my Prof. I couldn't cancel it."

Ruth thought that it was a greater effort for him to say this to her than to go out on to the stage and play the Moonlight Sonata to five hundred people. He looked far more nervous. She could scarcely believe that he had apologized.

"Clarissa is no more to me than the noise she gets out of

her catgut. I don't want you to think anything else, that's all." He looked better, having cleared this terrible hurdle.

"She was more once? I got that impression." She was so curious, wondering what had happened, as bad as her mother.

"Well, yes. You've only seen her being bitchy, but she's not always like that. She wasn't. Not last summer. Oh, cripes, let's not talk about that. People like that—and her mother—her mother——"

He looked harrowed, his eyes dark and scowling.

"I'm sorry, I don't want to know," Ruth said quickly. She wanted to know desperately, but not at the cost of such obvious pain to him. "It doesn't matter. Not now you've explained."

"I'm no good at explaining, that's the trouble. I can't talk. They—most of them—at college, they can talk, they know all the words. It doesn't mean they're any bloody good. But if you listen to them you think they must be. You—you must think I'm a pig, the way I am, but I can't tell you . . . I can't, how difficult it is, I mean. I don't want to—to—I don't want you to think I don't—I don't care. I——"

He paused, looking at her very earnestly, scowling. Then he gave a sort of groan and dropped his head and rubbed his hands through his hair.

"Cripes, it's hot. I must change out of this ruddy suit when we get to Northend."

Ruth was touched almost to tears. "It's all right," she said.

He gave her a very uncertain smile, and said, "Well, if you think so."

"The only thing is, I——" Ruth wanted to get it over, now that Pat was in an explaining mood. If this one thing could be cleared up, it would be moonlight indeed. "If it's not to do with Clarissa—I'm not being nosy, but I want to know why you got sent to . . ." She faltered, suddenly scared to death. "Oh, God," she thought, "why ever did I start?" She looked at him, appalled. "The three months . . . ?" It came out in a whisper.

"I hit someone," he said. "I broke his jaw and his parents got me hauled up for it. His father was a barrister—I didn't know that when I hit him."

Ruth did not ask any more, but after a pause Pat said, "He was one of the talkers, like I just said. He could talk about it—you'd think he'd sat there and told Johann Sebastian just what to put, the way he carried on. But when it came to doing, he was pathetic. He never did any work and he had the technique of a Grade One schoolgirl. He didn't like me, because I was going with Clarissa and he had an eye for her. He used to make remarks—he was very witty, he could always get a laugh, and it was easy for him—the way I talk, and when I was a waiter for a bit—he could take me off. I didn't mind about that part, but there was a competition, and I came top and he came bottom, and one day he was talking like *The Times* critic and I said if a piano was played with the tongue he'd got so much practice in he'd have come top—it was the only clever thing I'd ever said in my life, and he didn't like it. He said I put so many hours in because technique was the only thing I had to offer, my working-class brain being incapable of understanding what the whole thing was about. So I hit him. He was in hospital for a fortnight, and his father made sure I paid for it. So they got the last laugh after all."

Ruth thought it was a marvellous story. She said, "The satisfaction at the time . . . it must have been gorgeous! Even if afterwards——"

"Afterwards was different," Pat said. "It wasn't worth it. Not for all sorts of reasons. But at the time you don't think. All you think is, 'I'll smash that beggar,' and it's done. Even my hands—it didn't make any difference that time, although it's stopped me a few other times when I've been tempted. I couldn't play for a week afterwards. The old

Prof. was more wild about that than anything. And old Bigmouth—he couldn't talk either. That part was okay."

Pat's mood changed as if, having put both work and explanations behind him, he was all clear to enjoy himself. When they got off at Northend, he went and changed out of his suit back into his jeans and sweater, handed the bag in at the Left Luggage office, and came back to Ruth more cheerful than she had ever seen him.

"Now, what is it? A meal? Are you hungry? Maxwell said he was going to the Big Top and on to the Black Cat disco afterwards—would you like that? Cripes, it's hot! Let's have a drink first! You fancy that program?"

"Yes, oh yes!"

He took her in the station bar and bought a pint of beer and a shandy, then they went out and walked down the High Street to the front. The air was very close, although the sun was low; there was no breeze, and the tide was out, a mile away across the wet, puckered mud. The front was crowded with people, fat bare arms and peeling shoulders, tired babies bawling in their push-chairs, and lines for ice-cream. Ruth, who hated it usually, preferring it in the winter when it had a peculiar gaunt fascination all of its own, loved it tonight because Pat took her hand and said, "You're okay, Ruth. You don't nag. I don't like naggers."

"You like doormats?" she said.

"That's right." He grinned. "All the females I've ever known have been naggers. Except Mrs. Bates. And you."

"I'm quite a good nagger, if I put my mind to it."

"You don't practice enough. I don't believe you. The only thing was when you said this afternoon, 'I'm distracted.' You threw me. I nearly started on the old concerto instead."

"Yes, well, getting me up there—I could have died!"

He laughed. "I didn't think you would do it. But you never said anything. You never complained."

"You could have turned the pages yourself!"

"Yes, of course. But it was lovely having you there."

She laughed. "Catch me again! Not next Saturday——"

"Oh, cripes, next Saturday! It's all in the brain-box for next Saturday."

They turned in at the Big Top, into a steaming atmosphere of fish and chips and defeated salads under plastic covers.

"We should have had it in Hampstead," Pat muttered. "Let's collect Maxwell and find somewhere else."

Maxwell was at a table in the window, drinking coke with a girl who was introduced as Rita. Pat obviously knew her well. She looked at Ruth curiously. She was older, Ruth thought, as old as the boys, and she had a sophisticated command of the situation which Ruth envied, very casual and friendly, but sharp with it. She was not particularly attractive, but she certainly knew how to enhance what charms she possessed. Ruth felt cautious towards her, not wanting to reveal how unsure she was herself, her unsureness emphasized by the comparison.

"God, it's hot," Pat said. "And the ruddy tide half-way to France. I'd rather have a swim than fish and chips."

"Have a coke," said Maxwell equably.

"Let's go for a drink and get some cockles," Pat said. "Hey, wait a minute." He got up suddenly, threaded his way through some tables, and started talking to a youth who was sitting alone with a cup of coffee.

"He's very cheerful tonight," Maxwell remarked. "What've you been doing to him?"

Ruth smiled. "I don't know." "Not nagging" wasn't a very good answer.

"He must be in lerve," Maxwell said, winking. "Who's he talking to? Who's that bloke, Rita?"

"Len," said Rita.

"Who's Len?"

"Works at the baker's, where Penn used to."

"Oh. You going to this concert next Saturday, by the way? I know it's Penn and all that, but is the nervous system capable of standing a couple of hours of that sort of stuff? Mine—I doubt it."

"Oh, yes," Rita said. "We're all going. We're going to talk about him in loud voices and impress people. Our friend and all that. I saw Mr. Crocker last week, and he was babbling on about it. He said if you see Pennington, tell him Mr. Marsh has bought a ticket."

"Cripes, with real money? For old Penn!" Maxwell, for some reason unknown to Ruth, was convulsed.

Rita said to Ruth, "Mr. Crocker was the music-master at school. He's a decent old beggar, but Marsh—cripes, we all hated his guts. Penn most of all. He was always pitching in to Penn, but Penn got his own back in the end——"

"He got expelled for the pleasure, mind you," Maxwell put in.

"It was worth it," Rita said.

"Old Marsh'll be sitting there willing Penn to play wrong notes. You'll feel all the old hate-waves on the back of your neck," Rita giggled.

Pat came back with Len in tow, and Rita said, "Hullo, Len. I say, Penn, old Marsh has bought a ticket for your concert."

Pat scowled and said, "I hope they only had expensive seats left!" Then his expression went back to normal and he said, "Len's just taking me up to the bake-house and I'll get my old van. Then we'll have transport for the evening. Simmonds is on holiday so we're in the clear. Len's lending me his key. I'll be back in ten minutes."

"Good," said Maxwell.

"When d'you get your license back, Maxwell?" Rita asked him.

"Another couple of months."

He ordered another round of cokes, and Pat was back before they had finished, honking outside because there was nowhere to park. They all went out and piled in.

"Let's go and have a beer," Pat said. "Then we'll go down to the Lido and have a swim and then we'll go to the disco."

"The Lido'll be shut," Rita said. "It shuts at eight."

"It doesn't matter," Pat said. "We know how to get in, don't we, Maxwell? It's better when it's shut. You're game aren't you, Maxwell?"

"Yes. Suits me."

"You girls can sit it out. We won't be long."

"Catch me swimming," Rita said. "When are you going to grow up?"

"Next Saturday'll put ten years on me."

"High time," Rita said.

They stopped at a pub and the boys had beer, Rita had a martini, and Ruth had another shandy, leaving most of it. She wasn't used to drinking, and couldn't stomach any more. The day was very strange already, without the help of alcohol. They drove along the front to the Lido, and Pat parked the van in the first gap he could find, some way beyond. The pool was boarded up from the promenade, in order that prospective spectators should pay for admittance instead of getting free entertainment by leaning over the railings, but Pat and Maxwell led the way around to the side, ducked beneath a big billboard advertising an aqua show and, nicely screened by it from the people walking along the front, Pat climbed very nimbly on to the roof of the changing-rooms.

"Come on, you girls. Give them a bunk up, Maxwell."

Rita made a lot of fuss, but was hauled up without ceremony, very concerned for her tights. Ruth managed more easily, but was happy enough to have Pat's hand to help her. They slid down the roof to the other side and dropped down on the concrete sundeck. Maxwell pulled out two deck-chairs from beneath a pile shrouded with a tarpaulin, and set them out for Rita and Ruth.

"There, what more can you ask?" He offered Rita a cigarette and lit it for her, the match showing suddenly how dark it was, the warm sky close and thick with cloud, no stars showing. Ruth sat down, hearing the scrape of her chair echo around the blank façades of the changing-rooms. The big pool lay very still below, rank with chlorine. It didn't attract her with its chill breath, its occasional blink of stray reflected light a crocodile's eye in the darkness.

"Nut-cases," Rita said. "Keep your pants on in case you have to run for it."

Ruth couldn't reconcile it with the afternoon, the formality of the Hampstead fund-raising, and now the horseplay on the side of the bath, the two figures wrestling, overbalancing, Pat's fall turned by a twist into a smooth dive and the stillness splintered, the crocodile's eye fractured . . . She leaned her chin on the cold balustrade, wondering about the strangeness of the way things happened, the waywardness of one's feelings, so that there was no knowing . . . not anything . . . she was as dependent now for her happiness on Pat's whim as he was dependent on the buoyancy of the water for keeping him afloat. It wasn't at all a desirable state of affairs but—conversely—the new-found fragility of everything that mattered was the sweetest thing that had ever happened to her. She saw the glow of Rita's cigarette-end, and wondered if Rita had such feelings.

But Rita only said, "That should cool 'em off. They really are nuts." Her eyes kept going, somewhat nervously, to the promenade above. Maxwell came back, and lit a cigarette from Rita's and sat on the top of the steps smoking, until he was dried off. Then he stood up and bawled, "Come on, Pat! You going to be all night?"

He started to pull his trousers on.

Suddenly a strong beam of light flashed down from the promenade, transfixing Pat where he lay floating on his back in the middle of the pool. Ruth saw the startled expression on his face; he turned over and swam smartly for the side, the light following him.

"Oh, cripes," said Rita. "Here we go. Get Pat's clothes, Ruth. Where are they, for heaven's sake?"

The light swung around, and focused on Maxwell hopping about half in his trousers, and Rita scrambling for her handbag. Someone shouted, the voice resounding like a trumpet in a cave.

"What is it?" Ruth jerked out of her dreams.

"The coppers," Rita said. "We have to run for it."

Pat came running up the steps, half laughing, half in earnest.

"I've got your things," Ruth called. She was petrified, not knowing which way to turn. But Pat caught her by the wrist and said, "Come on. Down here." Maxwell and Rita were already away. There was a flight of steps at the end of the terrace, and at the bottom a door which Maxwell had already unbolted. Pat was laughing.

"Is it all right?" Ruth asked him.

"Yes, of course. Watch it—the steps are rotten."

The door gave on to a wooden flight of steps that ran down to the beach. Ruth stumbled down behind Rita, and Pat jumped over the rails and was waiting at the bottom, taking the bundle of clothes from her. They ran up the sand, Rita floundering as she lost a shoe, Maxwell shrugging into his shirt. The light picked them up again and a voice bellowed, "I'll have the law on you!"

"I thought it *was* the law," Ruth said.

"It must be the pool man. They say he does a patrol on hot nights."

"There was a copper," Maxwell said. "Let's keep moving. I saw him."

They climbed on to the promenade, the boys bunking the girls up first. Ruth rolled over the railings, getting tangled up with a pram and two children eating candyfloss. Rita had a fit of the giggles, hopping about trying to put her shoe on. The pool man gave another roar, mostly swearing, and everyone on the promenade stopped and stared, amused by the diversion. A policeman, not running but walking very briskly, was coming down the promenade from the direction of the pool's pay-box.

"Okay. Hurry up!" Pat said, and ran for the van. They all piled in, and Pat had it out neatly nosing into the stream of traffic while Maxwell was still slamming the door.

"Ruddy spoil-sports," Pat said.

"Lucky you had your pants on," Maxwell said, grinning.

Ruth, pressed hard against Pat in the front seat, and feeling herself growing rapidly cold and damp, was calmed by the collective indifference of the other three to their brush with authority. They were amused, sorting themselves out, Rita cursing because she had left her cigarettes behind. They stopped at some traffic-lights, and Pat reached for a cloth in the glove-locker and towelled his hair. A man in the car alongside gave him a hard, curious stare.

"What now?" Rita said.

"Eat," Pat said. "That's given me a nice appetite."

"I suggest you get dressed, before we all pile out in the High Street," Maxwell said.

"Yeah. Who's sitting on my clothes?"

They all were, and dragged them out with difficulty. Pat turned off down a quiet residential road and pulled over to the curb. He got out, pulling his jeans behind him. A woman came out of the door of the house opposite and came down the garden path, dressed to go out. She gave Pat a horrified look and said, "Really! I've a good mind to call the police!"

Pat cursed, turning his back on her, and Maxwell leaned out and said, "Yes, I would, madam. It's worse than the television. He's on the stage, and stage people are given to running around with no clothes on. If you want to see him, next Saturday at the Pavilion he's got his own show——" Rita hit him with her handbag, nearly knocking him under the dashboard. Pat zipped up his jeans and leaped back into the van.

"You raving twit, Maxwell!" The van shot off down the street. Rita was helpless with laughter, shaking against Ruth's shoulder. Pat could not find the gear lever for knees, and swore again. At the next red traffic-light he struggled into his sweater, and at the next one he combed his hair, peering into the driving mirror.

"Where are we going then?" he said to Maxwell when he had put the comb away. "I fancy some real food."

"The Golden Cockerel is all right," Maxwell said.

"Okay."

The Golden Cockerel was smart and cheerful, with pop music and a wine waiter. They ordered chicken, and the boys ordered beer, and lagers for Rita and Ruth. Pat's knee came up against Ruth's under the table, and stayed there, hard and comforting. She did not move away.

After the meal they drove down to the disco. Ruth had been there several times before but never with anyone that mattered. Pat parked the van in the street outside, and went to buy some cockles because he said he was still hungry. Maxwell and Rita disappeared inside, and Ruth waited for Pat while he ate, leaning against the wall outside the disco.

"You all right?" he asked her. "Want some?"

"No, thank you. Of course I'm all right."

"I don't know what you're thinking half the time. You just look and don't say anything."

"I'm thinking I'm very happy. I'm sorry—shall I nag you?"

He threw away the cockle bag and reached for her hand.

"So am I," he said. "And even if you nag me it won't make any difference. I wish it was like this every day."

They went into the hallway through the bright lights and into the vibrant gloom beyond, into a cocoon of noise, of intimate anonymity, body to body shifting and weaving through the slowly revolving beams of colored light. It was hot and the noise hurt, the rhythm seizing the knees, urgent and primitive, impossible—in the willing mood of pure happiness—to resist. They started to dance, laughing, very easy. Ruth had thought that Pat, steeped in classical music, would not be much of a dancer, but she saw that the argument was ridiculous: he had more rhythm and movement in one foot than most of the boys had in all their sweating, flailing bodies. For all his size, he was lithe and agile: Ruth's past partners paled into a limbo; she laughed, and Pat sang the pop words, the rubbish that now was as right as the sonata had been earlier, carefree in a way she had never seen him before, taking her, pulling her close, his hand on the back of her neck among her hair, singing in her ear and laughing and, as the pulse of the music quickened, turning away, pushed into movement by the compulsion of the noise—Ruth, too, getting breathless—and their eyes linked all the time, changing color in the revolving lights. Ruth saw Pat's eyes green as emeralds and diamonds of sweat sparkling; she saw his purple hair and the psychedelic lobe of an ear showing beneath, orange locks curling on the nape of his neck as he turned away to give the gaze a rest, the blood growing restless. Ruth felt the restlessness too.

The music changed, and the lights went half-down, the weaving slowed to a nebulous, hazy interchange, and the mood was changed. Ruth felt the heat, and the stirrings of her own instincts, charged and suddenly very painful. She looked at Pat, dazed and wanting, lost suddenly, and he pulled her close against him, one arm around her back and the other over her shoulder, the hand stroking her hair. She put her face in the hollow of his neck and touched his skin with her lips, and he moved her head back with the caressing hand and kissed her eyebrow and her temple and said in her ear, very softly, "Oh, Ruth, Ruth!"

"Pat," she said, stupidly. He was like a tower for her need; whatever it was she had wanted she had it in his arm holding her, and his body hard and warm against hers. She put her arms up and touched his neck and pushed the hair away from his ear, and heard the amplified voice singing out of the warmth and the bliss of love and pain and despair and comfort.

"You hear what he says," she whispered, and he kissed her hair and her cheek and said, "Yes," and kissed her lips, and smiled, looking at her, so close that she thought his eyelashes were almost touching hers. Her skin felt as if it were quivering all over. It was so strange, the other shoulders and hip-bones brushing them and swaying and shifting them about and they, a little cocoon, dancing very slowly and the sad voice washing them. The first shock of it past, Ruth was overcome with happiness. She dropped her head, seeing the glint of the gold medal he wore and feeling the warm roughness of the chain on her cheek where it ran over the ridge of his collarbone.

She thought she saw Maxwell grinning. Pat's fingers ran down her jawbone, lifting her head up.

"Ruth, I want——"

And then there was something else, an intrusion.

"I want a word with you." Another voice, not Pat's. Ruth came up off Pat's breast, blinking. A policeman stood there. She thought she was dreaming.

"If you'll just step off the floor a moment——"

"What for?"

"You'll find out."

Ruth, still in Pat's arms, looked up and saw his face unbelieving. His arms loosed her, and his hand took hers, very tight so that it almost hurt. Everyone was looking now, still dancing, grinning.

"Come on. We haven't all night," the policeman said.

He was an older man, very sure of himself. Pat hesitated, then shrugged, and moved away, glowering, still holding Ruth. They went out to the side of the floor, by the doorway, where another policeman was standing, an unsmiling hard-faced man. Ruth recognized him as the one who had stopped Pat the night outside the bakery. She felt a strong fear grip her, so strong that she shivered.

"This him?" the policeman asked Mitchell.

"Yes. That's him. Pennington," Mitchell said.

"I want you to step down to the station with me, Mr. Pennington," the policeman said.

"What for?"

"I'm charging you with taking and driving away the vehicle KRW 618E, the property of the Parade Bakery, without lawful authority."

Ruth saw the young policeman smile. Pat loosed her hand and hit him, with such velocity that she wasn't aware of its happening, except for the expression changing on Mitchell's face, his eyes glazing and his jaw sagging. The older policeman put out an arm, but Pat evaded it with a flick of his body and was out past him into the hallway. The policeman

bawled something and was after him, and Ruth found she
was there too, although she had no conscious awareness of
moving at all. She found she was standing on the top of the
steps, looking out into the street, and screaming. The hall
bouncer had tackled Pat outside, and two policemen who
had been waiting in a patrol car had jumped out and run
for the scuffle. Ruth saw Pat break out and run again, but
one of the policemen made a dive and caught him by the
arm.

"He's knocked Mitchell out!"

Pat was swung against the wall, the three policemen con-
verging on him. Ruth heard his head hit the bricks from
where she stood, and then the thud of a blow, and another
one . . . She started to run down the steps, but could not
move. Someone held her, and she turned around, pulling and
sobbing.

"Shut up, you fool! *Shut up!*"

It was Maxwell, shaking her silly. "I'll slap you!" he
hissed, furious. "Do you want them to take you too?"

"They're killing him!" She jerked at his hand, but he
tightened his grip, wrenching her towards him. His other
hand came up with a sharp slap across her cheek.

"They'll take you as well! You were in the van too! We'll
all get done if you don't shut up———"

She gasped for breath, shaking. "I want to go———"

"For God's sake," Maxwell said. "Are you daft?"

A crowd had gathered, craning and muttering. Ruth
could see the policemen bending over Pat on the ground,
and the crowd pushing in. She wanted to shut her eyes, but
they stayed resolutely open; she wanted to turn away, but
she could not move. She saw the crowd part, and the dark
figures straighten up. They had Pat between them, support-
ing him and holding his arms twisted up behind his back
at the same time. He appeared to Ruth to be barely conscious, his legs dragging, stumbling across the width of the

pavement, dark threads of blood running down his shoulder where his jersey was torn. One of the policemen opened the back of the van; they pitched him in bodily, head-first, and slammed the doors on him. The crowd broke away, and the policeman who had apprehended Pat in the first place came back up the steps of the disco, smiling and slapping his hands together. The two patrolmen got back in the van and drove off.

"Maxwell!" Ruth turned to him, all the strength drained out of her. Her voice was a whisper.

"Count yourself lucky," Maxwell said. "Me too. Let's get out of the way for a bit. Mitchell's lying in there, out cold —he saw us at the pool—it was him, you know, I saw his face under the street-lamp. He'll have recognized me, I'm sure. Let's go before he wakes up."

He put an arm round Ruth's shoulders and held out a large handkerchief, propelling her into the street at the same time, walking briskly.

"Cheer up, sweetheart. Here, mop up. Pat'll be all right. Don't worry."

"He isn't all right," she wept. "Didn't you see what they did to him? I thought—I thought—policemen weren't like that——" she hiccuped into Maxwell's handkerchief, shaking with sobs—"Not British policemen——"

"For God's sake, Ruth, what d'you expect them to do? He'd just laid one of 'em out cold, and was making a bunk for it, wasn't he? He wasn't going to stop if they'd said, 'I say, hang on a minute, old boy.' Pat's got a punch like dynamite. They weren't risking any more."

"What'll happen to him? Can't we go and see?"

"I can tell you without going to see. He'll be locked up and charged with stealing and assault."

"Stealing!" Ruth stopped in her tracks and stared at Maxwell in amazement. "That wasn't stealing!"

"It is to them. What we call borrowing they call theft."

"But he's not a thief!"

"No? You tell them that."

"But that's terrible!"

"Yeah, and knocking out a policeman doesn't endear any-one to the beaks either. I can't see him getting away with it, not with his record."

"Oh, Maxwell, you mean——" Ruth could not say any more for crying. It was the moment in the wings on the Hampstead stage, when she had been afraid: it had caught her up and overwhelmed her. She heard the thunder of the arpeggios and saw Pat's face again, fierce with concentra-tion, remembering how the fright had twisted her, and he had asked if she felt all right. The tears streamed down her face.

"There," said Maxwell, embarrassed but strangely tender, giving her shoulder a comforting shake, "don't cry. It'll be all right. He always gets by. He's used to trouble."

"I love him."

"Yeah, well, what's he got to worry about then? He's lucky."

"What will they do with him? Now, I mean? When he gets to the police-station?"

"They'll charge him, and get him to make a statement, or whatever they call it, then they'll put him in a cell for the night."

"Then what? Tomorrow?"

"Well, you're either let out on bail or remanded in cus-tody."

"What's that? Remanded in custody?"

"They send you to a prison, until your court case comes up. I think they send 'em to Brixton from here."

"Oh, God! How awful."

Maxwell didn't say anything, but steered her into a little café, sat her down in a corner and brought her a cup of strong coffee. Ruth didn't say any more. It was still so close, she could feel Pat's hand on her hair and his eyelashes brushing her skin. She saw his hands, very strong and agile as she had watched them all morning, and his expression changing with the music, his involvement making this invisible barrier that kept her from following, that kept her apart, waiting for him to come back. She would never follow him there, and he had made it his whole-time occupation. It was all very useless. And the part of him left over for her was this difficult, tangled, lonely, and undisciplined nature which by its crying need for support endeared him so much to her; and so uselessly, because she was in no position to help him, being as tangled herself and immature in her emotions as a fledgling caught against a window-pane. The coffee stopped her crying, but did nothing more to help; her feelings were too anguished and confused to cope with.

"Can't we do anything to help him?" she asked.

Maxwell said, "No," very firmly.

"What about next Saturday? They won't keep him for that?"

"I don't know."

Maxwell got up. "Come on. We'll go back and find someone to drive you home."

Ruth followed him. There was a boy called Crombie he knew, who was persuaded by circumstances to leave the disco on this errand of mercy. He had an old, rattling Morris Minor with a top speed of thirty miles an hour. Ruth sat in the back and half-heard them discussing Pat, laughing and amused. She kept thinking of him loving her, and his arms holding her, and him smiling and his lips touching her, and then hearing the thuds of the police hitting him, and his head against the wall. She was past crying, feeling that her own particular world had stopped, although everyone else was carrying on as if nothing had happened at all.

"Cripes, old Mitchell getting his desserts like that! I bet he's sorry now!"

And they laughed, and turned off the arterial down a side road, seeing a rabbit's eyes like green lamps in the road.

"If you had a gun, you could pot 'em easy as anything," Crombie said. "They just stand there."

"Yes," said Maxwell. "We ought to try it. My brother's got an airgun."

Chapter Seven

✹

She slept very late, having taken until dawn to fall asleep, and was woken by her mother calling, "Ruth! Guess who's here? A nice surprise for you!"

She sat up very suddenly, and the black memory hit her like a physical blow between the eyes, so that she lay back again and groaned. By daylight the confusion was cleared; the story was merely stark and sordid, and Pat a thief and a thug to be punished by the perfectly correct machinery of the law. Yet the sun was shining and there was a smell of coffee and warm grass. It was a perfect Sunday morning. And Pat would be stiff and sore and in despair and no one to help him. She remembered the words of the song they had been dancing to with perfect clarity. And she was lying in bed and shortly to take her breakfast, and her father was oiling the lawn-mower, and her mother singing. They didn't know anything of what had happened and she had no intention of telling them. Was it really as bad as she had thought it was last night? She dressed very slowly, pulling on her old jeans. Yes, she thought, it was. She didn't know what to do. The only thing she knew without any doubt at all was that her mother must not know what had happened.

Ruth looked at her face in the mirror as she combed her hair. She had a splitting headache and she was very pale, but at least she did not look as if she had been crying. She must be very clever, and aloof. Her mother would think they had had a row.

She washed and went downstairs and into the kitchen. The room was full of sunlight, making her blink, and in the doorway stood Peter McNair, holding her own gorgeous Toad. The pony had both front feet inside the kitchen, and stood there looking like something out of a legend, the sun turning his coat to pure gold, his friendly familiar eyes taking everything in. When Ruth came in, he gave a little snort and a flutter of his nostrils and Peter laughed and said, "You old flirt!"

"Oh!"

Ruth was quite overcome. Why, she had no idea, except that Toad and everything he stood for was so dear and familiar, and now seemed so far-distant and impossible—it was a terrible pang like homesickness.

She went up to him and buried her face in his lovely flaxen mane, quite overwhelmed. Her parents were laughing at her. The smell of Toad was as comfortable and kind and desirable as anything she could think of in the world. And so remote from everything that beset her. He was no good to her any more. It was terrible, now, trying not to cry.

"The vet's given him a clean bill of health, and it was such a super morning I thought I'd bring him down," Peter said. "He goes just like he ever did. Shall we turn him out?"

"Yes. Put him away and then come back and I'll give you some breakfast," said Mrs. Hollis.

Ruth walked down the back orchard with Peter, ducking for the old pear branches, watching Toad snatching at the grass. The grass was all wet with dew and full of buttercups. It was like a hundred years ago, Ruth thought.

"Is something wrong?" Peter said.

"Yes."

She told him, while they took off Toad's tack and opened the gate and let him loose in the big flat field that gave on to the marshes. The sky was full of skylarks. They hung over the gate, Peter chewing a stalk of grass, just as dear and familiar as Toad. She could tell him everything. They had been through all sorts of dire confrontations since the age of eleven, both on and off horses, and she knew Peter. He had his troubles too, but he wasn't a hysterical twit like herself; no one ever knew when Peter was troubled. He was very quiet and shrewd. He leaned on the gate, watching Toad move away through the wet grass, the animal's long early shadow undulating from the round white hoofs.

"You've really got it for this Pat, haven't you?" he remarked gravely.

"Yes. I love him terribly. And I know you're only being polite not making any remarks about how unsuitable he is for me and all that. I know you think that, but you must understand it doesn't make any difference. And that's why I must help him, because he hasn't got parents who are going to bother, like most people. In fact, I bet nobody but me and Maxwell know where he is at the moment. And nobody will care—even Mrs. Bates will just think he's stayed in London."

"But what can you do to help him? The police just do it all according to the book. You can't change it. Anyway, quite likely he'll be out this morning. They don't keep everyone, surely? They charge them, and then you appear in court later. And in between times you carry on just as usual."

"You mean he might be out by now?"

"Yes. I think they just keep you long enough to cool off, and then let you out. Unless it's something really bad."

"Oh, heavens, I must find out!"

"Ring up the police-station."

"Yes, of course. Oh, golly, it helps, just talking about it. I feel better already. Let's go and ring up the police-station. We'll go up to Ted's and use his phone."

"Have breakfast, or your mother will suspect something."

119

"Oh, yes. She mustn't know. She disapproves frightfully of Pat as it is, and this would finish it."

"Why doesn't she like him?"

"Because he doesn't say please and thank you and his hair's too long and his parents aren't nice and he's been in prison before."

"Has he?"

"Yes. But only for hitting someone."

Peter grinned.

"My mother wants me to go out with Gordon Hargreaves," Ruth said.

"Cripes!"

"Somebody nice. Or you."

"I resent being put in the same category as Gordon Hargreaves. Very much."

"Golly, yes. I didn't mean that. I'm sorry."

Peter smiled, and they went and had breakfast. Ruth took two aspirins when her mother wasn't looking. She felt very nervous and on edge, and the toast stuck in her throat. They walked up to Ted's neat new house, and hammered at the door. Ted put his head out of the window, very tousled, and came down.

"It's Sunday," he said. "S—U—N—D—A—Y. The day of the long lie-in. Or didn't you know?"

"Please can I use your phone?"

"Yes." Ted had a telephone for his work, as sometimes he was called out at night to take a breakdown truck to an accident. Ruth envied him his telephone, but her father wouldn't have one. "Who wants to pay for being disturbed?" he said.

Ruth looked up the police-station number in the book, and told Ted what had happened.

"Oh, cripes, your lover's a nutter," he said. He looked serious. "That's bad, Ruthie. Do the parents know?"

"Of course not."

The phone was ringing at the police-station, and she felt ill. Her fingers were shaking. Ted went into the kitchen and put the kettle on, and Peter picked up the newspaper off the mat and sat on the stairs reading it. Someone said, "Northend Police-station."

"I want to know—I—I'm asking about someone called Patrick Pennington."

"A missing person?"

"No. You've got him. I want to know what's going to happen to him."

"Patrick Pennington?" The voice went dim, talking to someone else. She heard it laugh and she caught the word Mitchell, and someone said, "Your coffee, George." A typewriter clacked in the background. Then the voice came back and said, "He's being remanded in custody. He'll be going to Brixton tomorrow. Who is that inquiring?"

"Ruth," Ruth said.

She put the receiver down, and sat looking at Barbara's wallpaper, green and gold squiggles on a lumpy fawn background. She saw Pat's face, and the way it had looked in the colors from the disco ceiling, very close to hers. And all her inside felt as if it was turning over with the pain of what George had said.

"They're taking him to Brixton," she said.

Neither Ted nor Peter smiled. They went into the kitchen and Ted poured out the tea and Ruth tried not to cry.

"Now what?" she said to Peter bitterly.

Peter shrugged. "I'm sorry," he said. "It didn't help at all, did it?"

"I suppose, if they're keeping him," Ted said, "someone ought to tell these music people, who think he's going to play in this concert of theirs. They might get him out, if they've got a bit of authority on their side." ·

"The Professor," Ruth said. "He would help him. Pat was going up to his place on Monday—tomorrow. Perhaps we could ring him up?"

She thought furiously. The Professor was the man to take charge. She didn't even know his name, let alone his address. Clarissa would know? She must ring up Clarissa and find out. Clarissa was in the London telephone directory, which Ted hadn't got.

"What do you do?" she said.

"You ring inquiries and ask for the number," Ted said.

Ruth went back to the telephone with her cup of tea. She sat on the floor, which was where Ted kept the telephone, and found out Clarissa's number. She rang it. They were a long time answering and she supposed they were all in bed. Perhaps it was the maid's day off.

Clarissa's mother answered.

"Pat's professor? It's Professor Hampton, dear. He lives in Chelsea somewhere. I don't know where exactly, but I could find out from Clarissa. She's been to his place. Wait a moment." There was a long, long pause. Ruth hoped Ted didn't pay his own telephone bill. But Mrs. Cargill-Smith came back with both the address and the telephone number. Ruth wrote it down. "Is anything wrong, dear?" Mrs. Cargill-Smith asked, but Ruth was already ringing off.

She rang Professor Hampton's number, her heart beating very hard and making her breathless. Another long, long wait. Then a woman's voice.

"Professor Hampton?"

"Professor Hampton won't be back until late tonight. He's in Paris just now."

"Oh."

She rang off. He would be back in time to meet Pat in the morning, but Pat wouldn't be there. She would go instead, and tell him what had happened. She put his address in the pocket of her jeans.

"You do choose 'em, Ruth," Ted said.

"I can't help it." She could have added, "Hark who's talking!" but didn't, being under Barbara's own roof. She told them what she was going to do, and Ted said, looking worried, "Ruth, are you sure he's worth——" and stopped, seeing her expression. Peter said, "If that's all we can do today then, how about coming home and you can try the new hunter Dad's got? She's super." And Ruth, to keep out of the way of her parents and have her mind distracted, said, "Yes. Very well." And for the rest of the day she felt that she was operating as two distinct persons, the Ruth that galloped Painted Lady through the McNair pastures, the sun hot in her face and her physical self gorgeously content, and the Ruth that was a little white ghost of the night before, terrified by what had happened and her inability to cope, and anguished by the thought of what Pat was going through. The contrast was so stark it was hard to believe that it was real, the emotions so torn that she came back feeling drained, as if she had had a whole day's hunting. Peter was kind, as Maxwell had been kind, but the whole thing was her own, and they couldn't make it any different.

The next morning she went to London, telling her mother she was going to Northend for the day. The journey was a nightmare with her anxieties and not knowing the way: she arrived at the Professor's front door and rang the bell with the feeling that she was a desert nomad arriving at an oasis. The house was in a Chelsea square, Georgian and pretty and immaculate; the area had a local, almost a village feel, with women shopping at the top of the street and an old lady walking her dog.

The door opened. A tall, middle-aged man with a stern, handsome face regarded her without smiling.

"Professor Hampton?"

"That's right," he said.

"If you're expecting Pat," she said, "he's not coming. Please may I speak to you? Something awful has happened."

"Oh, no!" said the Professor, closing his eyes and clutching his forehead. "Don't tell me . . ." The concern, although dramatic, was no act. There was no glimmer of a smile. Ruth saw a stiffening, a pulling-together in preparation for bad news, from what had been initially a cordial enough attitude.

"You'd better come in," he said. "I shall need a drink, if it's as bad as you say. Where is he?"

"In Brixton."

"Oh, my God, not again! Oh——!" The man groaned out loud. He gestured her inside, and Ruth stepped over the doormat, feeling that at last she was with someone who was going to suffer as acutely as herself, if for different reasons. The Professor shut the door behind her and said flatly, "Walk on—the door on the right. Oh, my God, the fool . . ."

The room on the right was large, and mostly filled by two pianos. Shelves crowded with books and piles of music lined each wall and there was a tape-recorder on the floor and a tangle of wires, and one armchair pulled up beside the fire-place.

"Sit down," the Professor said, gesturing to the chair. "Tell me all. He hit someone again? Who are you? A girl-friend?"

He gave her a stern, close look, and poured himself a whisky from a bottle on the mantelpiece.

"Do you want one? No? Some coffee?" He went to the door and shouted to the nether regions for some coffee, and came back and stood with his whisky, looking down at Ruth. "Tell me."

She told him, briefly, mentioning the concert, and Clarissa, and taking the van, leaving out the swimming and how Pat had kissed her.

"Assaulting a policeman . . . Is the boy mad?" The Professor was moved almost to incoherence. Ruth could see that he was a somewhat forbidding character, and sensed that his nature was austere and reserved, not easily given to the sort of despairing rage she was now a witness of. An elderly housekeeper brought in a tray of coffee and biscuits, and Ruth saw her surprise at the Professor's expression.

The Professor said to her, "It's Patrick, Clemmie. He's in trouble again. Can you believe it? After all we went through before——"

"Oh lor," said Clemmie. "Never! Oh, dear me, the poor boy! And him coming along so—oh, dear me, sir, what a blow!" Her face was all genuine concern. Ruth felt strangely comforted, that there were other people, after all, to whom Pat mattered. All her panicky feelings faded, and Pat took on a new dimension, another facet showing itself through the Professor's concern. This Patrick was not the boy eating cockles, saying he wished it was like that every day; this Patrick was the stranger in the dark suit at the keyboard, the one who went where she could not follow. And yet, in this room, he seemed unaccountably close. She felt very much better.

"You can do something?" she said. "You can get him out for next Saturday?"

"Well, God knows. I couldn't stop it before, could I? Three months he got, and all I could do was send a piano down there in a furniture van and they let him do two hours before lights out, after a day spent mixing concrete or something. If that was the sum total we could achieve last time——" He shrugged. His face was tight with anger. He walked up and down the room, jingling some money in his pocket. "I have never, in all my years of teaching, come up against such a paradox as this boy. In some things, musically, he is quite astonishingly civilized—are you musical?" His glance snapped at Ruth and she shook her head. "Do you know anything of——? No. Well, I won't bore you with what you won't understand. In music he has an intuitive grace, in the very best sense, and in his behavior he can be so graceless that it is hard to credit. Do you understand me? Do you know him well? How long have you known him?"

"Not very long. But I know what you mean."

"You do?" He gave her another very searching look. "Do you find him such a mass of contradictions as I do?"

"Yes."

"I have always thought that his life here—his musical life—was smoothing his natural aggression. I must have been wrong. The very first time I met him he was on his way to the police-station to be charged for something—I forget what. It seems we have progressed no farther. He disappoints me bitterly."

His face was so stern that Ruth began to wonder whether Pat would find much joy in a visit from his tutor, even if it was in order to secure his deliverance. She began to understand something of the pressure Pat worked under; she did not think the Professor was an easy man to please. She tried to explain the personal element in Pat's brush with the law, his long-standing acquaintance with Mitchell, in order to put his sins in a slightly better light, but the Professor was not mollified.

"To hit someone at all, considering his vocation, is imbecile. To choose a policeman is wanton. And to do it a week before a concert of the importance of this one on Saturday is——" He broke off with a gesture of complete disgust. "There are no words to describe it." He glanced at his watch. "I must go down to Brixton and see how things stand . . . get hold of my lawyer . . . there must be no question of his being unable to play next Saturday." He gave Ruth another of his keen glances. Ruth sensed that he

126

wanted to know the relationship, how much of a competitor she was for Pat's attention.

She said, "He's been working very hard for this concert. All day. Every day."

"Not, I hope, with you in the vicinity?"

Ruth was cut by the man's meaning, and colored up with indignation, but was too nervous of him to say anything back. She shook her head. She saw Pat lying on the sea-wall, the water glittering on his face, the Professor's influence binding his desire, darkening his expression . . . or was she being fanciful? She hated the Professor.

The Professor said, "It is essential that he works hard at this stage. Don't you understand that?"

Ruth lifted her chin stubbornly. "Yes, I do understand it. And he does work hard. I've never met anyone who works so hard. If you think I get in the way, you are wrong. The only times he has ever taken me out, it has been to concerts. Even on Saturday—it was to a concert, and practicing all morning first."

The Professor looked surprised at her tartness, and softened slightly.

"Good. Very good. I'm told he played very well on Saturday. I'll put it down to your influence."

Ruth could not tell whether the remark was meant kindly or sarcastically. The Professor continued, "Occasionally, in this job, we get a student who makes everything worth while. Patrick is one of those. Unfortunately, he has personality problems that are apt to overwhelm us at times, as you can see. I knew this when I took him on. I considered the risk and have not, until now, regretted it. I tell you this because I want you to understand that I do not take this trouble with all my students. With quite a lot of them, I feel six months sewing mail-bags would make very little difference to either them or me. But for Pat, it is another matter entirely. For example, I would not presume to give advice to the girl-friends of any of my other students, but to Pat's I would say, 'Do not waste his time.' Do you understand me?"

Ruth understood him very well. She did not reply, feeling too bitter to trust her voice. Her lips very tight, she stared into her coffee-cup. So much for her journey, she thought; she had accomplished a good deal more than she had bargained for. She saw her own fingers tighten on the cup-handle, and remembered hurling one of her mother's cups at the wall at home only a week or two earlier. She could well have done the same with the Professor's, the way the anger caught her, the indignation swelling like a physical pain. She put the cup down and stood up and went to the door.

"If I hadn't come, no one else would have told you what had happened to him. There isn't anyone else," she said. Her voice shook dangerously, and she knew she would cry if she said any more, so she went blindly out to the front door. Unfortunately, the latch had an automatic lock on it, and she could not get it to open, and had the humiliation of being forced to wait for the Professor to do it for her. He came out and put his hand on it, and she waited, back to the wall, her face stony with trying to hide the rampaging of her thoughts. But the Professor gave a bleak smile and said, "Yes, I'm very grateful. Thank you very much." He opened the door a few inches, and held it.

"Are you coming to the concert on Saturday?"

She was forced to look at him.

"Yes," she said.

"Then you will see him there. Don't worry, my dear. Things have to be said. The situation understood. Then we all know where we are. Don't be angry."

He let the door go and she went out, stumbling down the

128

steps into the street. He was sympathetic, but she did not look back, the resentment too strong, shaking her. She thought he was inhuman, ruthless . . . *unkind*. He cared very much about the Pat that produced music, not the Pat that was a human being. "Personality problems!" Ruth muttered furiously . . . all Pat's frustrations and difficulties and deprivations rolled into social-worker's jargon, getting in the way of his career . . . the phrase speared her. And then, souring and confusing still further, she remembered that Pat liked the Professor, respected him. He had said so. He was prepared to accept the Professor's standards; he had turned away from her on the sea-wall because of the Professor. But on Saturday night he had forgotten.

Ruth had no idea where she was, hurrying along a crowded street, muttering and scowling, all bound up in such a confusion of thoughts that she saw nothing. Her thoughts got her nowhere; there were no conclusions, they were so wild and undisciplined and prejudiced. Her anger left her, and she was hungry and her head ached.

And then, staring unseeing at her own reflection frowning back from a boutique full of black leather dresses, she wondered if Pat had meant what she had thought he meant on Saturday night. The doubt came like a jolt out of the blue, fixing her to the pavement. Or was it the beer and the dancing and what all boys did, moved by the moment, quite meaninglessly? In Brixton, moved by a very different atmosphere, he might well not have given her a thought at all. How did she know? Why had she taken it for granted so glibly that he might love her as she loved him?

"Oh, God," she said, staring at the straw eyelashes on the shop model, hypnotized by the horror of this revelation. "He wants it to be like the Professor wants it. He's as good as said so. Even Saturday—the disco—was only a reward to pay me back, for protecting him from Clarissa. And kissing me like that—" Was she so old-fashioned, so naïve, so antediluvian, that she thought it meant anything? Had he ever shown that he cared tuppence, sought her out, been jealous of her, even held her hand with the damp, trembling passion of Gordon Hargreaves? No, not any of those things. Only the offhand affection for not nagging, the routine pressure of a knee under the table. There was nothing. "Oh, God," she thought, the tears bursting up, the shop-window dissolving, "I am so infantile, so stupid, so dumb, so *feeble!*" Even the crying, a wet rag, not knowing anything, where she was, what to do . . . she was so *pathetic* . . . no wonder she did not move him. Everybody kissed everybody all the time without the sky falling. She was a nineteen-ten girl, straight out of the nursery.

She did not remember getting home. She remembered, at Northend station, that Pat had left his suit there, and she got it back, after a lot of argument and the intervention of the station-master and a phone call to the police-station.

"Whatever have you got there?" her mother asked.

Ruth said, "Pat's suit."

She remembered all the things that her mother mustn't know, surfacing from her stupor.

"He left it at the station on Saturday night. Then we forgot it."

"I'm surprised to hear he possesses one," Mrs. Hollis said.

"He doesn't wear jeans for concerts," Ruth said scathingly.

"Are you all right?" her mother asked. "You look peaky. All washed out."

"Yes, I'm all right." She went upstairs and hung Pat's suit on a hanger. It was a beautiful suit with a Simpson's label. There was nothing in the pockets save a handkerchief and a diary. She looked doubtfully at the diary, and riffled through the pages very rapidly, to see if there was anything in it. She knew that if there was, she mustn't read it, but did not know whether her frame was up to such restraint. She very much doubted it. But the diary was empty except for, every few weeks, the name or names of some pieces of music and the name of a place. She assumed they were concert engagements, and confirmed it by looking up the following Saturday. It said, "Northend. Rachmaninov C Minor under Backhaus. God save us." There were no girls' names, no girls' addresses, neither her own nor anyone else's.

Ruth lay on her bed and looked at the ceiling.

The week passed. The posters for the concert, both in the local newspaper and in Northend remained uncorrected as to the soloist for the concerto, and Ruth assumed the Professor had achieved Pat's freedom. She heard nothing, and could not bring herself to ring up the Professor. She did not exist, she thought, not for them nor for herself. She was just a walking, eating thing, mooching down the field, going for long, slow rides on Toad and lying in the grass looking at the sky, going shopping and forgetting what she had gone for. She thought of Pat the whole time.

Her mother, with magnificent restraint, asked her no questions. Only, "I take it we're all going to this concert on Saturday?"

"Of course. He gave us the tickets, didn't he?"

"Yes. I just thought you'd dropped out with him or something."

"He's in London all this week."

"Oh, I see."

On the Saturday morning Ruth got up early and went to Northend, with the suit. It was an excuse, if she needed one. Her mother had washed the white shirt, which had been crumpled, and ironed it, and it lay on the top of the suit which her mother had expertly folded. Her mother's part in it made it seem that Pat was accepted—now, when there were more reasons for her to reject him than ever before, did she but know them. The homeliness of the washed shirt touched Ruth, so that she had quickly to think about something else, to keep herself from buckling again.

The Pavilion was on the top of the cliffs, set among the corporation gardens that were terraced down to the sea. It was a perfect September morning, very still and bright, and everyone about their Saturday business, brisk and unconcerned. Ruth walked between the ranks of geranium and cineraria, along the gravel, swinging the bag, praying. The Pavilion appeared deserted, gazing out to sea with its glass frontage aflame, its posters making a mess of the architect's intentions; a dust-cart was parked outside. Ruth went in the front door. A woman was washing a vast expanse of rubber-tiled floor, down on her hands and knees.

"Is there a rehearsal here this morning?" Ruth asked her.

"I think so, dear. Coffee for ninety-three, they said."

"Can I go in?"

"As far as I'm concerned you can."

She heard it, opening the swing door, a great sigh of strings. Thick carpet hushed her feet. She pushed open another door, and the music lapped her, embracing the whole theater. The stage was brightly lit but the auditorium was in semi-darkness. Ruth had expected it to be empty but there were quite a lot of people listening, several of the middle rows being almost filled up. Whatever they were playing, it was not Pat's Rachmaninov, for there was no one at the piano. Ruth walked down the gangway and sat down close to where everyone else was, and saw immediately that there was a group of about a dozen people sitting to one side down in the front. The conductor, a small man in shirtsleeves, turned around while he was still conducting and called out something to this group, and one of them said something back. The conductor put down his baton and the orchestra stopped playing, apart from a flute that wanted to finish its own particular bit. Ruth saw someone stand up and recognized the Professor; he went forward and the conductor came to him and they started talking. The members of the orchestra shuffled their chairs, changed their music, and started to chat, some of the strings tuning, and the people in the audience murmured among themselves.

"Now," thought Ruth, "I get up and walk down to the front and give Pat his suit."

But it was quite impossible.

Pat was with the Professor. The Professor turned and said something to him and he got up and went to join the discussion with the conductor. Then they all went up on to the stage, and stood talking for some time, leafing through some music on the top of the piano. Then the Professor went back to his seat and Pat sat down at the piano and everyone stopped talking. Ruth went cold and sick, as if she were going to play it herself, and shut her eyes. There was a long, long silence. Then, quietly, the chords she remembered, not nervous and stumbling at all, but rich and urgent, unrolling towards the waiting strings and the raised baton as eloquently as Ruth remembered it in the Festival Hall, surging into the great tide of melody, so that Ruth forgot that she was nervous and in despair, only marvelling that this was Pat, who had written "God save us" in his diary, who was no doubt in as deep a despair as herself, but yet was capable in his playing of making everything else but the music completely irrelevant. "It doesn't just happen," she remembered him saying, but now it did, or to Ruth it seemed so, sweeping her up on such confident waves of pure and beautiful noise that nothing else mattered any more. What had she expected? She didn't know.

What had he been worried about? She didn't know, the music taking her, wrapping her about with such tenderness that it was as if the whole past week of anguished uncertainty had never happened. She wanted to laugh and cry at once, like the ladies in the cinema who had watched the film. Oh, how she loved him! There wasn't anything else but this, and the music was all her feelings distilled and swelling the corporation dome, escaping into the lovely morning and the hazy September sky. Her heart filled her, pressing everything else into insignificance.

When it was finished, the little audience broke into a spontaneous outburst of cheering and clapping. The conductor turned around, smiling and holding his hand out to Pat, and called down something to the group of people in the front row. Ruth saw the Professor get up and go up to the platform, and the first violin got up and went and said something to Pat. Everyone started buzzing. Ruth got up and started to walk down the gangway, propelled by some force quite outside herself, and quite undeniable. She could not even feel her feet touching the ground. She went up to the edge of the platform, slipped between a pair of fat, solemn men talking in German, and called out, "Pat!"

He was still sitting at the piano, and the conductor was saying, ". . . We do this part again . . . where the clarinet comes in, or from the beginning of the movement if you prefer it. I feel we take it too slow from what you want. You say."

Pat turned his head and saw Ruth. His face, very taut and grim, seemed to Ruth to flower, the smile coming as she had never seen it before. He got up, leaving the conductor in mid-sentence, and came to the edge of the platform, and leaned down to her, holding out his hand.

"Ruth!"

Another hand, hard as a vice, clamped itself around

Ruth's elbow, and a clipped angry voice, directed at Pat, said, "Will you kindly remember what you are doing!" and Ruth felt herself moved off across the space in front of the seats and up the carpeted gangway as much by an implacable will as by the physical force on her arm. She went in a dream, Pat's smile lighting her, her feet feeling several inches above the ground. The Professor directed her through the swing doors and swung her around to face him.

"Go away!" he said.

Ruth smiled at him.

"When I said you would see him today, I meant *after* the concert. Never before. Do you understand?"

"I brought his suit."

"I beg your pardon?"

"His best suit. He'll need it tonight. It's in a bag on seat H ten."

"Oh." The Professor looked at her very closely, and Ruth saw him visibly soften. He almost smiled. Not that she cared.

"Don't you dare put your face through these doors again. Not until tonight. You will see him *afterwards*. I promise you. Now run along."

"But now, when he's finished . . . ?"

"He hasn't finished. He has only just started."

"But it was perfect."

"It was very far from perfect."

"Afterwards then?"

"He will be at my hotel, resting . . . having a bath, keeping his mind in order. Nothing you can help him with, thank you very much. Good-bye."

Ruth sighed.

But it was all right. She went, drifting past the geraniums and the cineraria, not seeing anything at all.

Chapter Eight

✸

Sitting squashed in the back of her father's car with Ted and Barbara, on the way to the concert, Ruth didn't think that even Pat could feel more nervous than she did herself.

"They've given him bail then?" Ted asked her, out of earshot of everyone else.

"They must have. I don't know."

She should have asked the Professor what had happened but in her dream this morning she had never thought.

"You haven't told them? They don't know?" he asked, nodding towards their parents.

She shook her head.

In the car, she kept wondering if thoughts of her had intruded upon Pat's thoughts of Rachmaninov that afternoon. She was in competition with the Professor's ideals. It was still for Pat to decide, for she had neither the wish nor the will to put up a fight. She was done for.

"Barbara's going to have a baby," Ted said suddenly.

Mr. Hollis nearly drove into a telegraph pole. Mrs. Hollis gave a little shriek and turned around, clutching her seat, her face flushing up with strained pleasure.

"*Darling!* How lovely! Oh, how lovely!"

"Well, well, well," said Mr. Hollis.

Ruth looked at Barbara and saw that she was genuinely happy. Her usual peevish expression was changed to a self-satisfied glow. Ruth wondered if motherhood could work such a far-reaching miracle that Barbara would stay looking like this, that her character would be changed. Perhaps it was what she had wanted all the time she had worked and come home tired and had to cook the supper and nagged at Ted because he didn't wash up. It was what it was all about, after all. She thought of Pat and wanted to cry. The Professor didn't want it, not at all.

"Auntie Ruth," her father said, and laughed.

She tried to smile.

"Grandad," said Barbara. They all laughed like mad.

"This is a celebration then," Mrs. Hollis said. "How lovely! It really is the first time we have all gone out together since you two were married! That was very considerate of Pat, Ruth. He's going up in my estimation all the time."

Ted winked at Ruth, but with a gleam of sympathy. He recognized her feelings in the dark uncertainty of her eyes and the pale cheeks. Pat would go down in their mother's estimation a lot quicker than he had come up, they were both thinking, when she knew. Ruth stared out of the window.

Outside the Pavilion was a notice saying, "All seats sold." There was a crush of cars and people greeting each other, streaming in along the geranium walks, their best evening clothes rudely tossed by the breeze coming off the sea. They waited for Mr. Hollis to come back from parking the car, Ruth keeping apart, not wanting to have to talk. She was nervous of seeing Maxwell or Rita, and them saying something that her mother might overhear. But her father joined them and they went inside and took their seats. They were in the middle beside the gangway about five rows from the front. "Too close, if it's loud stuff," said Mr. Hollis, but Ruth thought, "It's close enough to see what he's thinking." Much closer than she had been in the morning. She could not believe that it was going to happen, in spite of all the evidence. There was a man on the stage putting music on all the stands. Members of the orchestra started to take their places, tending their instruments, blowing their noses and chatting quietly.

"Pity it's not Duke Ellington," Barbara was saying to Ted.

"What a gorgeous girl," Mrs. Hollis whispered to Ruth, and Ruth turned and saw Clarissa coming down the gangway with her mother. She turned back quickly, shrinking in her seat, and said, "That's Pat's ex-girl-friend. The one whose house we went to last week. She plays the violin."

"My word, but she's beautiful."

"She's horrible," Ruth said.

Her mother smiled. The chestnut hair floated away into some seats safely out of range, and Ruth relaxed. Clarissa still loved Pat, Ruth remembered; she saw Clarissa's expression across the lunch table, and heard the bitterness in her voice. What had happened between them? She wished——

"Good evening, my dear."

She turned around, and found the Professor easing himself into the seat immediately behind her own. She gaped at him, the color flaring.

"If you want to have a word with Pat afterwards," he said, "I'm warning you we shall have to leave as soon as he's finished. Like Cinderella, he has to be back at the gates of his other world on the stroke of midnight."

He smiled, all sweetness.

"But——" Ruth was panic-stricken. "I must see——"

"Yes, dear girl. You can come with me when it's over."

"Oh, thank you."

"Whoever's that?" her mother whispered.

"His Professor. His teacher."

"Whatever did he mean about Cinderella?"

"Oh, it's the way he talks. In riddles." "Oh, good lord," she thought, "suppose he talks to his companion about Pat being sent to Brixton!" Her mother was obviously going to listen to anything he might say.

But he was saying, safely, in reply to a question. "Yes, of course he's nervous, very nervous. But it would be amazing if he wasn't."

"Quite. Playing under Backhaus doesn't happen to many students. How did the rehearsal go?"

"Very well." They launched into technicalities and Mrs. Hollis said to Ruth, "What a distinguished-looking man! When did you meet him?"

"Last week."

"I must have got Pat all wrong," her mother said. "I just didn't realize . . . He didn't give me the impression that he was anything other than the typical offhand, mannerless teenager. I still can't quite believe this is going to be the same person that used to deliver our bread."

Ruth found it impossible to reply. Her feelings, assailed from all directions, were beaten to a numb, flickering mess of contradictory emotions, jumping like the nerves in a bad tooth.

She had expected Pat first, forgetting the overture. The eminent conductor received an enthusiastic reception which he acknowledged with smiles and waves more Gallic than Teutonic and launched immediately into something very soothing and lyrical. Ruth sat back and shut her eyes, wanting to be soothed, but the piece came to an end before she noticed any change in her feelings.

Backhaus left the stage to a storm of applause and Mrs. Hollis said to Ruth, "I don't know about you, but I'm quite nervous."

Ruth watched the members of the orchestra chatting again, and putting the Rachmaninov music ready. Somebody opened the piano up. The second violin turned up the corners of the music to make them easy to turn over, and

Ruth remembered that they only did it for their wages; they did it nearly every night, year in, year out, and it meant nothing to them at all. She didn't believe it.

The applause started again, and the conductor came out from the wings with Pat. Pat was in evening-dress, which shook Ruth—and evidently her mother too, for she gave an audible gasp—but walked to the piano with a scowl on his face that was familiar enough to counteract the unfamiliarity of the appearance. He gave the briefest of nods to the audience, an uncertain smile to the first violin, and sat down with a professional flick of his tails over the back of the stool. If he was nervous it didn't show, apart from the grimness of his expression. Backhaus said something to him and he nodded, and the violins all got ready to go with a communal movement that made Ruth think of the archers in some medieval battle. Pat rubbed his palms down his thighs, glanced at the conductor, who nodded, and Ruth leaned back, feeling all her tensions slipping away as the piano sounded out of the waiting silence. She could watch, feast herself on Pat, knowing that—whatever the Professor's opinion—his playing was flawless. He gave the impression of utter and complete involvement, without any anxieties at all, only a tenderness that Ruth had never seen except when he was at the piano; he was away, over her boundaries again, where she could not touch him, although he was physically so close that she could follow his every movement, almost as if she were turning the pages again. How could he remember it, she wondered? It was so complex and rich in its great profusion of sound, not clean and linear like the sonata last week, but a thing of eddies and surges with cascades of notes all sounding off to drown her again, as she had been drowned in the Festival Hall. It surely wasn't *easy* to do—it was "hours and hours for months and months"—and when the solo instrument threw in its lot with the whole orchestra and flung out the magnificent theme in virtuoso abandon against the soaring strings and brass, it looked to Ruth like very hard physical work, but the acceptance of it was effortless and total: it was wings lifting all the sour old pains into limbo. Ruth could have laughed out loud.

"My word, I would never have believed——!"

Between movements, Mrs. Hollis couldn't find words. Pat wiped his face and his hands with a pristine handkerchief and shifted the stool a fraction, and scratched his nose. Ruth remembered that at the same time last week they had been climbing over the roofs of the bathing-huts at the Lido. She sat there idiotically smiling, and the melody of the slow movement reached out and caught her off guard, very quiet and simple, a soft rippling of the piano over which the clarinet lifted the sighing tune; Pat played as if he was dreaming, very still and upright, taking the tune himself and meandering with it through a background of strings. It grew more urgent, the current taking it, swelling and falling over smooth stones, until, through flurries and long lilting waves of melody he took it all alone to its con- clusion, very grave and soft, with Herr Backhaus watching, sad and still. Closing, it left the listeners in suspension, not a murmur, not a squeak. Backhaus smiled. Pat dropped his hands and glanced at the conductor, not showing anything. He rubbed his hands over his forehead and pushed at his hair, then sat scowling, biting the side of his thumb-nail, waiting for the orchestra to gather itself to the raised baton.

Ruth heard the Professor say, "Biting his nails, my God!" but his voice was full of satisfaction.

Ruth thought she guessed why Pat was biting his nails, led by the orchestra into an altogether more restless in- volvement, his dream given over to a very businesslike con- centration. The now familiar melodies were charged with an urgency that had not happened before; Ruth sat back, pushed, enslaved by the noise. "Hackneyed," she remembered. Clarissa would be wearying across the gangway, unless the fact that it was Pat playing had the power to unweary her. But the climax building up between the piano and orchestra stopped the silly wandering of her brain, shaking her, stopping her from everything but a pulsing participation. It was impossible to be detached as the piano climbed the scale and ran down again in spectacular figures that Ruth could put no name to, while the orchestra soared up on the last outpouring of the marvellous tune, the piano crying out underneath until, faster and faster, it cascaded to the final thudding halt with chords delivered by Pat with the whole of his very considerable strength in exact accord with Backhaus's cutting-off gesture with the baton. That it might have been otherwise would have been disaster, but that it happened with such breathtaking perfection left Ruth limp with a sense of utter completion, gorged in every one of the faculties which had earlier been in such dire need of refreshment.

The applause was immediate, almost a carrying on of the music's thunder. There were shouts and stampings and a storm of clapping. Pat got up, looking stricken, and the conductor came around and put his arm around him and shook his hand, and Pat remembered the procedure and smiled, and went and shook hands with the first violin, and then he stepped forward and bowed very correctly to the audience, dropping his head so that Ruth noticed the gash among the hair which he must have got in hitting the wall last Saturday.

Mrs. Hollis fortunately noticed nothing but his elegance in the formal black suit, for she said to Ruth, "Magnificent! Gorgeous! I still can't quite believe it!"

The Professor leaned over to Ruth and said, "Are you coming, my dear?"

They walked out together through the noise, shutting it out through a padded door. They climbed some steps and went up on to the side of the stage, seeing it all from a fresh angle, the backs of the double-bass players and the cellos, and the piano far away, its lid yawning. The Professor was smiling.

Ruth said, "It was perfect, wasn't it?"

"It was all right," he said, and smiled again. "Promising," he said.

Pat came off with the conductor, his face quite expressionless. Whether it was Brixton or whether it was Rachmaninov, he looked to Ruth a good ten years older than when she had last seen him, exactly as he had promised Rita. Perhaps it was the suit. The Professor went up to him and Ruth knew that it was only his conservative upbringing that stopped him from embracing him. As it was, he put an arm around him and said something Ruth did not hear. Ruth, watching, felt a small pang of jealousy. Whatever the Professor said, Pat would take. Whether it was about Rachmaninov or about girls.

The applause was still tumultuous. Backhaus was shaking the Professor's hand and laughing, and Pat took a comb out of an inner pocket and combed his hair very carefully, and wiped his face and his neck with his handkerchief, and Backhaus did the same and they went back together to take another bow.

The Professor turned to Ruth and said, "Pat has the very precious gift of being able to produce more, the bigger the occasion. The more it matters, the more nervous he is, the better he plays. There are many unfortunate, and equally gifted, musicians who would give almost anything to have this particular—well, what is it?—quirk of nature, perhaps? Showmanship, if you like. It is terribly necessary to a concert pianist."

"Oh," Ruth said. She didn't want a concert pianist. She wanted Pat.

After the second bow he came to her, while the Professor

talked to Backhaus. He put his arm around her shoulders and gave her a little squeeze, but did not say anything. In a strange way it was as if he wasn't there at all; it was as if a current of electricity had brushed her. His eyes had seen her, but his brain was not connected; it was away where she could not move it. Curiously, she was not upset. It seemed perfectly in accord with the occasion; even she was not immune to the vibrations, shaken by the fading trail of Rachmaninov's glory through the dusky, gold-lit haze of the auditorium. So how could Pat, who had made it, come down so soon? Backhaus, more practiced, took him by the elbow and said, "And again, my friend. Again." And they went out to take another bow, and Ruth thought how strange it was that there was nothing there, once it was done. Nothing at all. Like being a medium. And yet, even more strangely, it was just a job, born of long hours at a village-hall piano and lessons paid for by the Northend corporation. The enigma she had first sensed in the Festival Hall. The Professor was smiling, his austere face lit with what Ruth guessed was a rare excitement.

After the fourth bow there seemed to be a whole lot of people who wanted to see Pat. The members of the orchestra streamed off for the interval and Ruth almost got carried away in a black stream of German chat. When she had fought her way back to the Professor, she found both him and Pat talking to a little old grey-haired man who looked to Ruth as if he was close to tears. Pat called him sir, and seemed to be coming back to earth in his company, a faint smile breaking. The Professor introduced several very cheerful, well-dressed men, and then Mrs. Cargill-Smith and Clarissa and two or three boys who looked like students broke in, but Pat, Ruth noted, did not put his arm around Clarissa, but merely nodded and muttered something, and Ruth was content to have them say their piece and go.

At last, by dint of moving further in when someone else moved out, she found herself next to Pat. He turned away from a rather fulsome woman in black who seemed to be a friend of the Professor's, and looked at her very gravely.

"I don't know what I'd have done if you hadn't come," he said. "I've been thinking about it all the week—that you would be finished, after last Saturday. You haven't come to —to—say that . . .?" His voice was soft and uncertain, his face drawn and tired.

"No," Ruth said, "I couldn't stay away. I've been thinking about you all the week too."

He smiled as tenderly as if she were a little dreamy piece of Rachmaninov. Ruth, strangely, remembered the Brahms waltz in the village-hall. Her own smile was out of control, all over her face.

"It's what happened before," Pat said. "And I was so scared it was going to be the same. This last week has been awful—not knowing about you. Not the other things. I——"

"If you're going to hear the rest of the concert, you'd better go and take your seat," the Professor said to Ruth. Everyone else had vanished and the orchestra was all ready and waiting again, and Backhaus emerging out of the doorway to the dressing-rooms.

"She's not," Pat said. "She's coming with us."

He took her by the arm and marched her through the doorway the conductor had just come out of. The Professor followed them. They heard the applause breaking out, like waves on a beach, and they were in a quiet corridor, the door closing behind them, the concert shut away. Pat opened another door and they were in a dressing-room; Ruth saw Pat's jeans and sweater flung over a chair, and the Professor's expression in the mirror, not angry, but amused and complacent. He was glancing at his watch.

"We've time," he said. "It's all right. You get changed, and we'll go and have a little drink. Sit down, Ruth." He pulled out a chair. "A little celebration, before we set off. I think we can consider we've plenty to celebrate just now, in spite of all the other problems that beset us. We'll forget them for the time being. He played very well, eh Ruth? Don't you think I'm a very good teacher?"

Ruth smiled cautiously, taking the offered seat. Pat took off his tailcoat and waistcoat, and his white tie and shirt and washed very splashily. Ruth, seeing the drops of water running down his back, remembered the sea-wall and the shadow of the Professor; she knew the Professor would not leave them alone together. Just as he had been there on the sea-wall. She got up and handed Pat a towel that was hanging over a rail, and he blinked at her through the water and smiled. She saw the little gold medal hanging around his neck and wondered if Clarissa had given it to him. He put his old clothes on and the Professor gathered up the suit and the odds and ends that were lying around, and they went out to put the things in the Professor's car. The breeze came up from the sea, sharp with the smell of the mud-flats and the seaweed under the pier, hinting at old wet timber and crushed crab-shells and whitened sticks and blobs of tar on the smooth pebbles. A ship was moving down on the ebb, its lights passing the pier, the soft thud of its engines like an animal breathing in the dusk. The water was calm, brimming beneath the first stars to the far shadow of the Kentish shore.

Pat watched the ship, and said softly, "Oh, God!" He kicked the wheel of the Professor's car, his hands thrust into his pockets. "What a ruddy mess! What a——" He shrugged, turning away.

"Come on," the Professor said sharply. "There's a pub across the road. We can spare ten minutes."

Pat took Ruth's hand, and they crossed the road and went into a cosy, dimly-lit pub with an oak-beamed ceiling and candles in bottles, and soft canned music, all very comforting and suitable. The Professor bought two double whiskies and a sherry, handing the sherry to Ruth. He pushed one of the whiskies to Pat and said, "We'll take you back happy. There's nothing in the rules against it, as far as I know."

Pat gave a faint smile.

"What's going to happen?" Ruth asked. "When will you know?"

"The case comes up before the magistrates on Tuesday," the Professor said. "It appears that it is almost certain that it will be adjourned to the Quarter Sessions, to be tried before a jury, and there is very little we can do save plead not guilty and try and get bail. We have hired a very high-powered lawyer who thinks he might manage this, as he managed—against all the rules in the book—to get Pat the day off today. If he doesn't manage, the next Quarter Sessions aren't for another month, so that Pat will disappear from human ken as soon as the case is over. And there will be nothing at all we can do about it. These minions of the law—they are quite immovable. The whole thing is completely out of our hands. British justice, unfortunately, is utterly irrevocable, absolutely implacable, quite ungiven to accepting the odd bribe, yielding to the sly hint! I have considered everything, even to putting in a plea of insanity."

"Thank you," Pat said gravely.

Ruth could not tell whether the Professor was really joking or not. She could not divine the Professor, the meaning of the gleam in his cold grey-blue eyes. Although he cared so much for Pat, it was not a fatherly care; it was a driving, implacable—his own word for British justice—care; it was something very stern, although it had love in it.

To Ruth it explained a great deal of Pat, and she now felt that it was this cold, caring pressure that made her own love for Pat by comparison so mushily, defensively emotional. Pat seemed so vulnerable suddenly, in spite of every apparent physical indication to the contrary—just another of the innumerable contradictions that so entangled him— that she felt of her own love now as entirely a giving, protective thing, to help him. She wanted nothing from him for her own comfort, but only to give it to him. Perhaps it was the sherry, but the feeling was so strong she could not have said anything sensible at that moment. Pat did not say anything either, staring into his whisky, turning the glass around in his fingers.

There was a long, thoughtful, sad silence.

Then the Professor said, "This was supposed to be a little celebration. For tonight. A very successful day, Pat, whatever else might or might not happen. Backhaus was very happy. Let's drink to that."

They drank, and the Professor started to speak to Pat about his performance. Pat, although he said very little, listened attentively and Ruth stood close beside him in a warm haze of her sherry, thinking that the Professor would carry on like this right to the gates of Brixton prison, dissecting, analyzing, shredding into little technical facts the whole fabric of what to Ruth had been a thing which words could not touch. Did he never let up at all? Ruth felt her expression hardening, impatient, and angry.

He glanced at his watch again, put down his glass and started to walk towards the door, still talking to Pat. They crossed the road back to the car-park and went to the car. The Professor unlocked it, got in and pushed the other door open for Pat.

"Get in," he said.

He started talking about the restatement of the second

subject in the first movement. Ruth put her hand on Pat's arm. The Professor started the engine.

"Pat," Ruth said.

Pat was holding the door, just getting in. He turned his head and looked at her, then straightened up again, retreating, letting the door swing to.

"Ruth," he said, "you must come back, afterwards. I can't—I can't——" He reached for her, pulling her hard against him. "Don't go away." She put her arms around him, frantic, lifting up her face. "No! Oh, no! I won't ever ——" He kissed her, stroking back her blowing hair, then, with what was almost a groan, pressing her head closer, kissing her again. His strength almost hurt, yet there was a tenderness, an asking not a demanding. Ruth felt herself lost, holding on to the hardness of the back of his neck, brushed by the softness of his hair.

"It's all right," he said. "It's all right as long as you don't go away." He kissed her again, very gentle.

"Pat!"

Ruth wanted to laugh, but she thought she was crying. The Professor was furious, revving up his engine. He pushed the door open. Pat straightened up. Ruth saw his eyes, lit by the electric street-lights, full of her own reflection, not thinking about the Professor at all. She laughed then, almost like crying, and said, "I love you."

"I love you too," he said.

"Do you mind?" said the Professor acidly.

Pat got into the car. Ruth saw the Professor's face, green in the street-light, filled with unstarry thoughts, lined, and grim. He let in the clutch and the car went away with a well-bred roar, very fast. Ruth walked across the car-park to her father's car, and sat on the wing, staring into the warm darkness. She was not real. She was away with the stars and the breeze off the water, holding Pat's kisses, filled with the sad urgency of his voice. Pat, oh, *Pat!* It was a pain and an agony and a happiness beyond words. She had never been kissed by anyone who mattered before Pat, and it occurred to her then that he was as accomplished in his loving as he was in his playing; he had practiced, she thought, with a sad diversion of her mind, recalling the puppy fumblings of the other boys, the clumsy advances, the unsubtle grabs. Never had she felt so right, so filled, so piercingly sure of anything as when Pat had held her, and she wanted to convince herself that the conviction of his caresses was prompted by love, not merely by plenty of practice. But he had said so. He had been torn and shaken, not teasing and amused. His face in the lamplight had been stark, almost fierce. "It is true," Ruth thought. "He loves me. He said so." She could not move herself from this fact, shivering on the wing of the car, held by the glory of what had happened.

The car-park, suddenly, was no longer deserted. People started to filter through from the park, spilling out of the Pavilion, talking and laughing. Ruth tried to come back to earth, and couldn't.

"Oh, there you are!" her mother said. "We thought you were with Pat. Whatever are you doing, all on your own?"

"He's gone. He had to go. It wasn't worth my coming back."

Mr. Hollis unlocked the car, and they all piled in.

"Whatever else he isn't, according to your mother, he's a very fine pianist. I must say, I thoroughly enjoyed that." Mr. Hollis put the ignition key in. "Okay at the back?"

"I think he's dishy," Barbara said. "Why was I always out when he brought the bread?"

"I shouldn't imagine he'll have to do that sort of job much longer. What's his program now? Has he left College?"

"Not yet."

"Why did he have to rush off then?" Mrs. Hollis asked. "He's not had to go back to London, has he? I would like to have told him how much we enjoyed it."

Ruth did not reply. Ted started to talk about something else, tactfully, and Mr. Hollis nosed the car out into the traffic. They cruised along the top of the Upper Promenade, looking at the lights below, and the great calm darkness beyond, which was the sea.

"You ought to invite Pat home one evening, Ruth. We ought to get to know him," Mrs. Hollis said. "He obviously isn't what I thought he was."

"He is what you thought he was," Ruth said.

"How do you mean?"

"He had to rush off because he has to be back in prison before twelve. Brixton. They just let him out for the concert."

She was past subterfuge now; she was not even afraid of saying it. It would be public knowledge on Tuesday, and what her parents might say, then or now, would not move her in the slightest degree.

Her mother gave a sort of groan and turned around, her face green and tight in the neon-lighting, with much the same expression on it as the Professor had revealed when he had driven away. Mr. Hollis changed gears with a crash and said, "Any more surprises tonight? Let's have them all while we're on the subject."

"There aren't any more."

"What did he do?" Mrs. Hollis demanded. "Why is he in prison?"

"He borrowed a car and when a policeman came and asked him about it, he hit him and ran away."

"When did this happen?"

"Last Saturday."

151

"You mean, when you were with him?"

"Yes."

"Oh, my God, Ruth, you mean you were involved in it? You might have landed up in the police-station too?"

"I might have, but I didn't."

"How dare he! How dare he put you——"

"He didn't! It just happened. He didn't plan it! He was sweet to me. It was the loveliest evening in all my life."

"It sounds like it! Dragging you into——"

"He didn't drag me——"

"Please," said Mr. Hollis. "Not tonight. Not after he gave us so much pleasure. Can't we talk about it tomorrow?"

"Yes," Ruth said. "I don't want to talk about it again. That's all there is. I've told you now. There's nothing else to say."

"Oh, isn't there?" said her mother, grim as the Professor. "That's your opinion, Ruth, believe me."

"Later," said Mr. Hollis.

"Yes," said Ruth's mother. "Very well, we'll talk about it later." And she stared out of the window, her face as black as the darkness over the sea.

Chapter Nine

✳

Ruth, as always, it felt to her, knew nothing, not even who to ask or where to go. She had had nothing to do with the law all her life; the village policeman was a friend, the only policeman she knew. This was Pat's side of it, this gaunt hall of echoing footsteps and brown doors, of worried people conferring, a woman crying, policemen everywhere . . . the smell of cold swabbed floors and brass polish. Every day, she had discovered: six courts sat every day, and she had passed the imposing civic building hundreds of times in her life with never an inkling of what it was all about. "So this is where I find out," she thought. She felt sick with nerves.

She went up to a policeman standing at the bottom of the flight of stairs that led up out of the entrance hall.

"Where do I go for—for—to hear my friend—er—tried?"

"Magistrates' court?" the policeman asked. "Or is it trial by jury? The magistrates' courts are upstairs. These two down here are Quarter Sessions. Each court has got the agenda pinned up outside."

"Oh." She thought back to the Professor, and decided that it was the magistrates' court. The Quarter Sessions were to come later.

"Upstairs . . . thank you. Will he be—be up there now?"

"Is he on bail or in custody?"

"In custody."

"He'll be downstairs in the cells then, till the case is called."

She climbed slowly up the stairs, not wanting to see Pat in a cell, even if it was allowed. The only cells she knew about were the big barred cells in Westerns, where the man inside got hold of the jailor through the bars and half-throttled him with one hand while relieving him of the keys with the other, and the pictures in the newspapers of new prisons, with flowers and pin-ups and the occupant with his face blanked out. Neither seemed relevant to Pat at all, yet he was in custody, and that's what it meant, bars and locks. She found it very hard to accept this fact, the whole experience of being outside the law completely beyond her narrow privileged world, where meals were always punctual, arguments were just grumbles, and crises no more than a pound note in the washing-machine by mistake. "I don't know anything about anything," she thought. Pat had done all this before; he knew the procedure, he knew what it was like to be in prison, to be pushed around by the screws. To her "screw" was a book word, in quotes, but to him it was perfectly familiar vocabulary. She supposed that, by the end of the day, she would be able to accept this alien experience; it would be part of her experience through Pat. Pat had caused her to grow up more quickly during the last few weeks than in all the other years of her life. Just for an instant, hesitating on the top of the stairs, she realized that all this had happened because of the instant's decision she had taken that day in the lane, to turn around and stop his van, and ask for a lift. "Suppose I hadn't?" she wondered. And the thought was exploded by scorn into instant fragments.

She was on another floor of brown doors and policemen chatting, and men in dark suits going in and out.

"Patrick Pennington," she said to a policeman. "Is this where he comes up?"

"I'll have a look, Miss."

It was there in writing, pinned on a board, half-way down a long list, "Regina *v.* Patrick Edward Pennington. Taking and driving away a motor vehicle without lawful authority. Assaulting a constable in the execution of his duty, thereby causing actual bodily harm."

"This room, Miss. Number two."

"How long will it be?" There seemed to be an awful lot of people in front of him.

"Can't say exactly, Miss. But a lot of these are very quick—parking offenses and such like. He'll be in before lunchtime."

"Can I go in?"

"Are you a witness?"

"No. Just a friend."

"You can sit anywhere at the back. Wherever you like."

Friendly and obliging, he waved her through the open door into an impressive wood-panelled room. There was a raised platform facing the door, with a long desk and three chairs pulled up to it with the town's coat-of-arms in gold on the dark leather backs. Below it was a long table with several of the dark-suited men chatting and setting out papers, all quite affable and normal. Several of the chairs around the room were taken by policemen and various nondescript people who Ruth supposed were friends and interested parties like herself. There was nobody she knew. The sun shone into the room through long windows overlooking a cemetery. It was another kind of September morning like the morning of the rehearsal, a day for lying on the sea-wall in the thick yellowing grass. Ruth saw Pat's brown naked back and his eyes watching her, the grass crushed down, his blue shirt flung like a patch of the summer sky. She felt crushed inside.

Someone bellowed, "Stand!" and everyone stood up, abruptly silent. The magistrates came in from a door at the back and took their places at the bench. The room seemed to fill up, and someone was shouting through the door into the corridor outside, "Call Peter James Anstruther! Peter James Anstruther!" Peter James Anstruther, a stocky man with long sideburns, came in and was directed to a chair just in front of Ruth, where he was charged with driving a car with defective brakes, treadless tires, and a broken headlight.

"Do you plead guilty or not guilty?"

"Guilty, sir."

Ruth was watching the magistrates. The middle one of the three, who seemed to be the one that mattered, was a woman. She was elderly, with a strong, lined face, an angular figure, and strong brown hands. "If I were her," Ruth thought, "what would I think of Pat?" But she could only think of the woman thinking, like herself, that Pat was marvellous. She gave Peter James Anstruther a fine of twenty-five pounds. The next man, for stealing a leg of lamb out of the supermarket, she fined fifteen pounds. Parking over the stipulated time, parking for fifty minutes on a yellow line, driving a motor vehicle with defective lights, using threatening behavior likely to cause a breach of the peace, drunk and disorderly in a public place . . . the men at the long table came and went, shuffling papers . . .

"The beer was dripping from the ceiling, and the mirrors were shattered. Damage was estimated at thirty-eight pounds . . ."

The man just in front of Ruth was a little, vague-eyed newspaper-seller.

"He's very sorry . . ."

A man came in and took a seat against the back wall. By his build and the way he walked, Ruth guessed he was Pat's father. He had the same thrust of the lower lip and the aggressive frown, the same cautious eyes. Ruth watched him, the nervousness thudding inside her.

"Relationships in this family are not entirely satisfactory. Mrs. Wilde's son said, 'I'll smash you with a bloody chair.' To which the accused replied . . ."

"Oh, God," thought Ruth, "how many people are there in trouble?" Pat was only one of countless thousands. Surely his case was no worse, no better . . . couldn't she say to Pat, the woman with the strong intelligent face, as she was saying to the miserable man facing her now, "I have every sympathy with your situation, but it is no excuse for this sort of behavior . . ." A fine wouldn't hurt Pat, but to shut him away when the sun was shining and the sea was coming up the beach over the warm sand and the trees on the crumbling sandy cliffs were yellow and gold in the still air . . . Ruth caught herself up in her mawkishness and shook her head.

"Fifteen pounds and five pounds costs."

The door opened again and the Professor came in with a man in a dark professional suit and a file of papers. Two policemen came and sat down next to Ruth.

"Call Patrick Edward Pennington!" the voice bawled at the door.

Ruth felt as if she couldn't breathe.

One of the policemen said to the other, "This is the young sod that broke Mitchell's ribs."

"If it had to happen, he couldn't have picked a better bloke."

"No. It won't do him any good though. Not with the new directives come through about tightening up on police assault."

Ruth looked anxiously towards the door and saw Pat come in with a policeman. He was wearing his best suit, the one Ruth had rescued from the railway station, and looked more like one of the lawyers than the accused, very serious, his face showing nothing, the lower lip pushed out slightly. He came across the room to the chair by Ruth, saw her, but made no acknowledgement. He turned and faced the bench, and the policeman stood beside him. The woman magistrate looked at him, and did not remove her eyes, while the man at the table, who seemed to do most of the talking, picked up his papers and found the right page.

"You are Patrick Edward Pennington?"

"Yes, sir."

"You live at 4, Church Cottages, Fiddler's End?"

"Yes, sir."

"Your date of birth——" He fumbled again, coughed, and found the correct place. "Your profession—I understand you are a music student?"

"Yes, sir."

He turned to one of the other men at the table, who Ruth had gathered was some sort of public prosecutor, and this man picked up his sheaf of literature and intoned in a parsonage voice:

"Patrick Edward Pennington is charged that on September the third of this year he did take and drive away a motor vehicle belonging to the Parade Bakery without lawful authority, and secondly that when apprehended by a police constable he did assault him thereby causing actual bodily harm."

He then said something to the man who had come in with the Professor, and turned to the bench and said in a normal voice, "I would formally ask you, madam, to take this case to trial at the Quarter Sessions."

The magistrate nodded.

"Is he on bail or in custody?"

"He is in custody, madam."

The Professor's lawyer stood up and said, "I would make a very earnest application, madam, for Mr. Pennington to be released on bail until the Quarter Sessions."

The magistrate looked at the prosecuting man, and he said, "The police oppose bail, madam."

A frown passed over the magistrate's face and she studied Pat thoughtfully. She then studied the sheaf of papers that had been handed up to her, presumably, Ruth guessed, describing Pat's offense, and the Professor's lawyer said, "His own Professor, Professor John Hampton, a director on the board of the College of Music, will stand bail for him, and will have Mr. Pennington to live in his own home until the trial comes up. I would add, madam, that Professor Hampton's interest in this student's circumstances is by no means trivial. It is an extremely unusual and tragic case, in that this trouble has come into this young man's life just when every opportunity is opening up for him in his career—as you would understand, madam, if you were present at the concert at the Pavilion on Saturday night when he played as soloist under the visiting German conductor, Otto Backhaus."

"I was present," said the magistrate.

"On the strength of that performance Backhaus has invited Mr. Pennington to play with him again when he returns to this country at the end of the month, and there is also an invitation for him to play in a concert at the Albert Hall at the end of the week, in place of the original soloist who has been taken ill. You will understand, in these circumstances, how very strongly I would advise that bail should be granted."

"This is not entirely to the point," the magistrate said. "He is no doubt not the first person to time his appearance in court at a very inconvenient moment for himself."

She turned and muttered something to the magistrate beside her, and the three of them had a short confabulation. Ruth looked at Pat, who was almost near enough for her to touch him, standing very still, his hands clasped behind his back. The magistrate stopped muttering and said to the prosecuting lawyer, "Who is the police officer in charge of this case?"

"Inspector Griffiths."

"And he opposes bail?"

"He does, madam."

The magistrate frowned again, and appeared to sigh. She stared at Pat, as if she would read his intentions, but there were no intentions written there. Pat looked back at her, his face congenitally defiant, the brows drawn down as they always were, the jaw set. But Ruth could see a pulse ticking in his neck, and his fingers moving restlessly, and the dampness of apprehension on the cheek-bone. "So would I feel," Ruth thought, "and the sun shining and the sea warm outside and everyone going for their lunch in shirt-sleeves, and the old ladies paddling . . . So do I feel." She found she was holding her breath, and it hurt, and she wanted to reach out for Pat. *Pat.* She shivered.

"Is Professor Hampton in court?"

The Professor stood up.

"You are willing to have this young man live with you until his trial at Quarter Sessions?"

"I am."

"Very well. Patrick Edward Pennington, I will remand you on bail in the sum of one hundred pounds, and you are to appear here to be committed to trial at the Quarter Sessions on the twenty-seventh of September . . ."

Ruth got up, because everyone else was moving and the constable at the door was shouting, "Call Arthur Percy Macintosh! Arthur Percy Macintosh!" Pat turned around, white as a sheet. He looked at Ruth and said nothing, but Ruth saw him in that instant as if laid bare—it was as if, in one fragment of a second, he had no defenses at all. He looked at her and it seemed to her that he was at the end, against a brick wall, quite alone. She saw immediately that, for all the lawyer and the Professor and his father and Mrs. Bates and herself, when it came to the thing that mattered there was no help at all: nor ever could be. What one did was one's own. It was a thought like a hammer-blow. And as quickly, it was gone, because his expression came back, his human shell covering up his soul, and Ruth thought that her own emotions had run away with her. Pat wasn't like that. She looked at him, walking beside him out of the room, and he smiled at her. She was mistaken, she thought. Pat could take anything.

"Clear the landing, please."

"Pat," she said.

He took her hand. His own was as cold as ice. They walked down the stairs, and the man Ruth thought was Pat's father put his hand on Pat's shoulder and said,

"Good on you, Pat! I'd have kicked up a ruddy fuss about being kept inside until today. Where've you been?"

"Brixton."

"What's it all about then? Mrs. Bates told us, and your mother wanted to come but I talked her out of it. Thought she might stand up and make a scene. What's the bodily harm charge? That's what they'll get you on."

"They say I broke one of his ribs."

"Should've broken the whole ruddy lot!"

"Yeah, well, it's nothing to what they did to me——"

"Well, you got a good lawyer on it, haven't you? And if you've got marks to show—you're slow, Pat! You ought——"

"Oh, cripes, Dad, you know they just stand up there and say you fell down the steps to the cells, or you walked into the door. You say they pushed you into the door and who's going to believe it? It's not worth the trouble."

"No, you can't win, that's the pinch . . . Good luck all the same. I'll drop in and see how you get on on the twenty-seventh. You'll get sent down again, I suppose!" He shrugged, and his gaze turned on Ruth. "You're not alone, I see. You got someone to hold your hand."

"This is Ruth," Pat said. "This is my father." The introduction was cold. Mr. Pennington said, "Pleased to meet you," and Ruth dropped Pat's hand to shake his father's.

"Very nice," said Mr. Pennington. "What happened to that gorgeous red-headed bird you——"

"For cripes' sake!" Pat glowered at his father.

His father glowered back. "Whether you're stewing in Brixton or doing a Paderewski in the Albert Hall, you're still my boy. I got a right to know things. You remember that. And you might remember us when the big money starts coming your way. You didn't learn to play that ruddy piano out of thin air, you know. Your mother——"

"If I ever have a ruddy penny to my name I'll come and stuff it down your——"

"Pat, Mr. Merriman wants a word with you."

The Professor edged in, his voice sharp. "If you'll excuse us," he said very politely to Pat's father, "Mr. Merriman has to get back to London."

Pat turned away to talk to the lawyer and Ruth was left with Pat's two father figures, eyeing each other cautiously, as dissimilar a pair as were ever likely to meet, pointing up the contradictions in Pat's nature.

Mr. Pennington said, grudgingly, "I'm sorry he let you down."

The remark surprised the Professor. He said, "He's never let me down in his playing. It's what makes all this other business so sad."

"Oh, well, he's young. He'll learn sense. It's too late for me, but he'll make it, I dare say. I'll be seeing you." He dipped his head to the Professor, and then to Ruth, and hurried away.

The Professor looked at Ruth and shook his head. "An extraordinary gentleman. He goes a long way towards explaining Pat."

"Like you," Ruth thought.

The Professor smiled. "You're still faithful, I see?"

"Yes," she said stubbornly.

"You realize, don't you, that next time he won't get off? Mr. Merriman thinks the very least he can expect will be nine months and a pretty steep fine. I can pay the fine, but I can't do the nine months. Will you still be faithful then?"

"If he wants it."

"You're a sweet girl," the Professor said, very smooth. "You're too good for Pat. What do your parents say about it?"

She did not answer. She suddenly felt that of all the influences on Pat's life, it was the Professor's that was the most baleful. The feckless unsubtle father seemed like a great draught of fresh air beside the Professor and his guile, the grinding pressure he brought to bear, his possessiveness.

She turned to Pat, who had come back to them with the lawyer at his side.

The Professor said, "How about lunch, Merriman, then we can see about getting back to London? We can leave the two young people to their own devices, if you've finished with Pat. I've no doubt they can entertain themselves for a couple of hours." He smiled his polished smile. "All right, Pat?"

Pat nodded.

"You'll be coming back to London with me, of course. Suppose you meet me at the White Hart, say, in two hours' time? Will that suit you?"

"Yes," Pat said.

"Very well."

They went out of the court-house into the sun, and the two men walked off towards the car-park.

"Does he own you?" Ruth asked bitterly.

Pat grinned. "He does at the moment, I suppose. I'm his hundred-quids'-worth."

"No. I don't mean that. I hate him."

"What's he been saying?"

"He keeps warning me off. As if I'm trespassing. As if you belong to him."

Pat frowned. "You don't want to take any notice."

"Well, I——" She shrugged.

"Look," Pat said. "It doesn't matter. It's just how he is. He wants everything his own way. He's a bully. If he wasn't I'd never have got so far as playing with Backhaus on Saturday. Well, with my playing, that's all right, I don't mind, but in this it's different. He's no claim on my personal life at all. What *we* want now, he's just got to take. So don't you worry. You stand up to him, and you'll find he's all right."

Ruth considered this and felt better.

"Is it true, what the lawyer said, that you've got to play in the Albert Hall or something?"

"Yes. At the Proms. On Friday. Whoever it was who was doing it has got mumps or something stupid, and they asked me. The Rachmaninov again."

"Do you mind?"

"Mind?" He looked at her curiously. "It's marvellous. Why should I mind? I'll be scared as hell, but that's something you just have to get used to."

"You said, after the last concert, that you wouldn't have to work so hard."

"Yes, I did. But I see now, there's always something else ahead, and if there isn't it means you're no good. Backhaus asked me if I wanted to play one of the Beethoven concertos with him next year—the end of next year. He's coming over for a sort of Beethoven marathon—Edinburgh and London. So—well, I suppose that's how it works——" He looked at her, not quite sure of himself. "You—look, in spite of what the Professor said, there will always be time for

164

you. You haven't changed your mind? What you said on Saturday—it's true? You wouldn't have come today if——"

"No, it's true."

He put his arm around her shoulder and she felt his fingers touch her neck and her ear, and caress a lock of hair. She didn't say anything. They were walking down the High Street towards the sea, the shoppers and the trippers jostling them.

"We'll go down the pier," he said. "I'll buy you an ice-cream. I love you."

"Yes," she said.

"I'm going to buy a pair of jeans first. I can't walk down the pier in this suit."

He let her go and went into a shop and she leaned against the window, facing the sun, waiting. It was very hot and she could smell the sea mixed up with the buses, and the perspiration and the fish and chips, and the smell of new corduroy out of the shop. "It's impossible," she thought. But it was true. He came out of the shop in blue denim jeans and a red cotton tee-shirt, and his suit in a carrier-bag. The jeans had a label on the back pocket saying, "Genuine Hee-Man Denims. 30 waist. 36 inside leg," and the tee-shirt said "Made in Portugal." Ruth removed the labels and Pat took her hand and they crossed the road where it fell away down to the lower promenade, and the sea took over from the High Street, blue and calm and shining.

"I must have a swim," Pat said, looking at it.

Ruth laughed. "You've got a fixation on swimming, a thing about it."

He shrugged. "Compared with all the other things, it's the only one that doesn't matter, where you're free. After concerts, and Brixton, and the Prof. and the fuzz—cripes, sometimes I just wish I'd been a farmer like old Bates' dad."

"You didn't think that when you just finished on Saturday night. You won't think it on Friday."

"No. If you've done it as well as you can—it's pretty good afterwards. The best thing of all, I suppose. Only you know that it's never good enough, and as soon as it's over you want to start work again. It can't ever be perfect, even if you live to be a hundred. I'm hooked on it now."

They walked down the pier, out over the acres of wet mud to where the sea started and the fishermen clustered on the rail. The pier splayed out, sideways and up and down, left to the lifeboat and right to the restaurant, straight on for the amusement arcade, and the sun-deck where the deck-chairs were out in soldierly rows and the couples sat with newspapers over their heads, gently dozing. The air was crinkled with the heat, distorting the distance. Pat bought two ice-creams, and led the way down some iron stairs into a dark echoing landing, where, once, the paddle-steamers had tied up and the passengers had landed or embarked. They walked through the clammy shadow and came out at the end on to a lonely wooden jetty with steps down into the water, where people came for speedboat rides. But the speedboat had engine trouble, and was on its mooring beyond the lifeboat shed, the engineers working on it with their shirts off and cans of beer on the foredeck, and Pat and Ruth had the little private jetty to themselves. The boards were almost too hot to sit on. Faint canned music drifted down from above and occasionally someone threw down a sandwich paper, or orange peel, and the sea-gulls wheeled around, waiting, eyeing Pat and Ruth with beady, greedy eyes.

"I think we'll be late for the Prof.," Pat said. "I feel it in my bones."

They sat side by side, eating their ice-creams.

"You can't believe it, after this morning," Pat said.

"Life is very peculiar," Ruth agreed.

"If I'd had to go back, today," Pat said, "I think——" He looked at the water, scowling. "I think I'd have hit somebody else. That prosecuting bastard."

"The one who said the police opposed bail?"

"Yes."

"Why did the police oppose bail?"

"Because they've got my past history. I absconded last year, and once before I—well, they don't like you, anyway, when you take a swing at them. They just want to make it as bad as possible for you. The magistrate didn't know all this, of course, but she guessed it."

"She doesn't know what you've done before?"

"No. If you plead not guilty, it's not made known until—unless—you're proved guilty. Then it's all read out, so the magistrate can decide what sort of a ruddy sentence to give you in light of all you've done before. It's all very *fair*."

"But the police know all along?"

"Yes, of course."

"Why did you abscond?"

"Oh, cripes, there's enough to bother about without digging up last year's performance. That lawyer buddy of the Prof.'s thinks I'll get nine months. Did they tell you that?"

"Yes."

"Do you mind?"

"Do *I* mind! What about you?"

"Yeah, well, by the twenty-seventh I shall have got myself in the frame of mind to go back. There's nothing else you can ruddy well do. But today I wanted to talk to you. Today was worse, in a way. I want to know, when it happens, what you'll do?"

He was staring into the water, not looking at her.

"I'll just wait till you come out."

"What'll your parents say?"

"They've said it already. It doesn't make any difference. I haven't noticed, the way you talked to your father, that *you* take much notice what *he* says."

"No, well, he's just a bum. But your parents are probably right, what they say."

"Are you talking me out of it, too?" She looked at him, shaken.

"Cripes, no! Can't you see? I'm just weighing up my chances—I mean, whether you'll be around when I'm back in circulation again, or whether this finishes it. You must see, it'll make a difference to what it'll be like when I'm shut up—cripes, Ruth!—can't you see what it means——"

"I've told you!"

"And when I come out I'll have—according to this Merriman bloke—about a hundred quids' worth of fine to pay back to the Prof. and I'll have so much ruddy work to make up—I won't be fit to earn anything for months. I've got to tell you this, Ruth—you must know all this—I mean, even when you've waited all that time, what good is it—for you——"

"Look, I'll wait. There's nobody else. There's only you. And when you come out, whatever happens—happens. I don't see that it's at all complicated. I thought you were going to have a swim?"

He was silent. She looked at him, and he turned his head and smiled. The reflection of the water lapped on his cheek, moving gently, a weaving pattern of light across his jaw-bone, touching his mouth.

"You're all right," he said.

ing her back against the steps, his face dark as it turned

The brightness of the water made her blink. She screwed up her eyes. He moved very close, twisting sideways, press-

away from the sun.

"You make everything sound very simple. I hope to God

it will be how you say. I do love you." He kissed her, his weight suddenly hurting, his arms holding her very hard. She could not move. She groaned, laughed, dazzled by the sun in her eyes and his loving her, and he groaned too, not laughing at all, and dropped his lips into the hollow of her neck, so that her face was full of his hair, soft and smelling of institution soap. She freed an arm, and brought up her hand, holding his head against her, feeling his eyebrow under her finger-tips, and his skull and his cheek, smooth one way and rough the other. A little piece of orange-peel fell on his hair.

"Hey, mister! The tide's coming up!"

A rolled-up sandwich paper fell on Ruth's head and bounced into the sea. She opened her eyes and saw a trio of giggling heads peering over the rail above.

"Oh, *Ruth!* If only——" His voice stuck, incapable. He lifted his head and stared at her. His expression twisted her.

"It's all right," she said. "It'll be all right."

"Will it?"

A large piece of orange-peel fell on her nose.

"Spit on them! Spit on them!"

"Oh, *cripes!*" Pat twisted around and let fly a stream of language. The boards thudded to flying feet. Ruth lay back and heard the water swilling around the wooden piles in the dark shadows behind them. Two little boys were walking down the landing towards them with fishing-rods. The water slapped to a passing wash, hollow and cold, and splashed idly up over the steps, and the little boys danced over the grating, chasing crabs. Their voices echoed and flitted among the saturated piles. Pat stood up and pulled off his new shirt and his shoes and socks, and dived in off the steps. Ruth saw him disappear, and sat up. He did not come up for what seemed to her a hundred years, long after she had pictured him drowned, and brought in by the motor-boat men, blue and still, and all the people clustered silent on the sun-deck, watching . . . She stood up, her eyes full of tears, and he surfaced some fifty yards away, very leisurely. She sat down, and he swam back to her, very easy and strong, and came up to the steps and lay there, holding the step where the tide had reached. Ruth took off her shoes and sat with her feet in the water.

"I thought you had drowned."

"What would you have done?"

"Oh, got some lunch, I suppose, done a bit of shopping, caught the bus home."

"You little——" He was smiling.

And, as if because he smiled, it was her turn now to be twisted, the self-control sliding away.

"Oh, why——!" She had to catch herself up, nearly choking, turn away, look into the dark shadows under the pier. He shoved off again, turning over, floating, watching her. With a considerable effort, she said, "That's no way to treat new jeans," and he said, "Yes, it is. It shrinks them." He was dissected, half dark blue, merging with the water, half golden brown, arms stretched out, all hard muscles. Ruth smiled.

"Do you do weight-lifting or something?"

"No. Only piano-playing. It's very good for the physique."

"It's what grew the hair on your chest?"

"Of course." He smiled back, his eyes screwed up against the sun.

Ruth felt she was back where she had started from, admiring the physical Pennington, the baker's boy with the scowl and the aggressive presence. It was only mere weeks since that was all he was. And now, what she had got into was altogether the most demanding situation she had ever

170

encountered, stretching her from bliss to despair in a moment, sweet and hard, funny and tragic, to extremes she had never known existed. But not dull. She felt stiffened, accepting it. Better, after all, however much it was going to hurt, that it had *happened*. It was what she had wanted, wasn't it? Watching him, she felt a fierce, jealous sense of possessiveness. The gold medallion lay on his chest awash in the furrow of his breastbone, catching the sun.

She said, "Who gave you that? Clarissa?"

He put his head up, the hair falling sleek and smooth. "What, this?" He reached for the steps, turning over, hitching himself on the one where Ruth's feet were. "Are you jealous?" He sat up, shaking back his hair, grinning. "Yes, she gave it to me, and swore eternal love until the day she died."

"Honestly?"

"No. I bought it in the Portobello Road. It's Beethoven. Look. He makes me play all the right notes when I'm wearing him."

She took it in her hand and looked at it. Beethoven had slightly the same expression as Pat, a truculent scowl. The medal was old and worn and delicate.

"It's my good luck."

"Were you wearing it that Saturday, the night you——?"

"I always wear it. I never take it off. I played well at Hampstead. What happened afterwards wasn't *his* fault. He's only for my work, not for when I'm out with my bird. That's not his department."

"What happened with you and Clarissa?" She let the medallion drop, glad that it had no female connections. She had no compunction in asking this question now.

He frowned. "I've forgotten Clarissa. It doesn't matter."

"She hasn't forgotten you, judging from the way she looks at you."

He hesitated, the expression darkening. His voice was angry.

"She should have thought of that when *I* wanted *her,* in that case. She took me up because I was the best student in our year, and she was in a position to choose. Let's face it, anyone Clarissa fancied had to be very strong-minded to say no. Those looks, and that home, and their piano, and Mrs. Cargill-Smith buttering you up, and her father one of the directors of the Royal Symphonia Orchestra . . ."

He paused, and Ruth tried to imagine Pat's initiation into the Cargill-Smith home: had Mrs. Cargill-Smith's reaction been anything like her own mother's?

"I wasn't their sort, but because I was good they wanted to know me. I think they sort of like to think of themselves as being patrons of struggling young artists, and if the struggling young artists are a bit off when it comes to saying 'How do you do?' with the right accent and using a knife for peas they think it's eccentric and amusing. Not like the ruddy Prof. who bawls you out for behavior the same as he does for wrong notes. You know where you are with him. But with Mrs. Cargill-Smith when you're so eccentric that you land up in a detention center, then that's going too far—she isn't amused any more. She doesn't want to know. You're not a person to her, you're just a status symbol in the musical rat-race. And when that happened to me, I wanted Clarissa pretty badly, but she retired, along with her mother."

"You loved her?"

"Yes. I thought I couldn't live without her at the time. When I got nicked she promised she'd come and visit, and that's all I thought about, day and night—shows how green I was! But when the day came she didn't turn up. She said afterwards she came as far as the gates and then she said it was so depressing she couldn't face it. She turned around and went home again. So I waited and waited, and she didn't come. Afterwards she told me she thought I'd understand how she'd felt. Well, she never knew what *I* felt. I never told her. I've never told anyone. Only that's the night I cleared out—I went to the nearest town and got blind drunk and in the morning they picked me up and carted me back—I didn't care whether I lived or died. But it cured me. I didn't want to know her any more, afterwards."

Ruth, appalled, said, "But did she want it how it was before? Or was she ashamed?"

"She was friendly enough, but I wasn't. It was pretty difficult because we had a lot of work to do together—she had a whole lot of engagements, and I wanted the money. We used to have the most tremendous rows—musical rows —sometimes we'd go on the platform not even on speaking terms. God, it was terrible—the poor music. So it all folded up. I don't know how it is with her now, but I've no feelings for her at all. We do the occasional concert if it's forced on us. That's all. And you saw how it is . . ." He shrugged.

"But her mother seemed quite well-disposed towards you. Has she forgotten?"

"If she has, it's only because I got myself some good notices, and things like that concert with Backhaus—that's why she's friendly again. She's a musical snob. It suits her now to forget last year, but she'll never make me forget last year, not if I live to be a hundred. I didn't know much then. I know now that there's people like her who want to be friendly for what you do, not what you are."

Ruth, considering the implications of this story, felt the weight of her responsibilities settle and take hold. It was almost an aging process. She looked at Pat, sprawled in the sun, contemplative, the eyes bitter . . . His stubborn streak of social irresponsibility, so out of keeping with the almost painful responsibilities he was prepared to accept in his work, exasperated her.

"You ought to have learnt—if it hurt so much!" She could not stop herself. She heard the nagging tone of her own voice and put her hand on his shoulder, not wanting to hurt him. "I'm sorry, but—oh, it's such a waste—if you go away! Why didn't you *think?*"

He looked at her sharply. "I thought enough to hit him in the belly instead of on his beaky nose, which I would like to have flattened all over his face. I thought that much, not to hurt myself for the concert." He frowned, the expression hardening, almost challenging. "I'm not sorry," he said. "I don't regret what happened, if that's what you're thinking. I'm glad I hit him, and, if I'm sorry about anything, it's only that I didn't do more damage."

"But——"

"Yes, I know what you're thinking—I'm going to pay for it, but it still doesn't make me sorry."

"It doesn't make sense."

"It does to me. They put the old psychiatrist bloke on you, and the social what-nots, the busybodies, and they try to tell you all this, and it's meaningless. You do it because——" He shrugged. "They just don't know. There's a lot of things—you can't explain. *You* don't know what it's been like for me—my parents—*cripes*, when I took Clarissa home! She *wanted* to, she insisted. You can't imagine— you can't tell these people how some things feel—any more than you could make them know how it feels in the middle of the Rachmaninov on Saturday night—it's not something you can explain. And sometimes I feel—oh, God, there's just some things you can't take. It wouldn't be any different, if it could all happen again. I can't tell you—I can't explain. Oh, hell . . . we'd better go, the Prof. will be raving."

He got up, gathering his things together, shoving every-thing in the parcel with his suit. They walked back into the damp, echoing shadow of the landing, Pat scowling and unhappy.

"It's going to be ruddy awful, I know. I shan't get any remission, I don't suppose—I'll never get through it with-out getting into some sort of trouble. As soon as you get in court—oh, God, the feeling . . . next time, it'll be a proper court with a dock and the blokes in wigs, and the jury in their best suits, and they'll stand up and do their ruddy spouting—it's all such a farce, the stuff they talk, it's noth-ing to do with what really happened. They don't know any-thing about what it was like, kissing you, and then that copper—for nothing at all—all so senseless, but they expect you to take it, yes sir, no sir. They can't go wrong, with their uniforms and God Save the Queen and the other clap-trap—Well, you can't expect—oh, cripes, it's useless . . ."

His voice echoed and faded into the slapping of the water under the grating, and they came out into the sun-shine and walked in silence up the steps. Ruth felt cold.

"I—oh, well, that's how it is. But it's no good telling you I'm sorry. You might as well know."

Ruth remembered his look in court, against the brick wall.

"Have you got a comb?" he said.

"Yes."

She found him one and handed it over. How could you tell what somebody else really felt, or how they saw, out of their own eyes? The innermost part was always one's own. She could not reach Pat there. She could only grope through his words, and try.

"I never talked to Clarissa the way I've said all this to you," he said.

He gave her back the comb. "Thanks." He padded along

beside her over the hot boards, the wet jeans leaving a trail behind him. His face was closed up, scowling, as if he had departed. Ruth felt suspended, nothing, a dust mote floating on his moods, unable to make her own progress at all. Where did this thing lead to? It was as unsubstantial as the shimmering air over the cliffs. It was nothing like the beautiful sure perspective of the pier running straight and true to the shore. She wished it was.

"You can keep my Beethoven medal," he said.

She was startled.

"I shan't need it in the nick," he said. "They take your things away. I don't want them to have him. I shall need him on Friday, then after that you can have him, until I come out. Then you will have to come and see me, to give him back."

"I would love to have it, but I will come anyway, not just to give it back to you."

"You say that now."

"I'll wear it all the time. I will come. I promise."

"We'll see," he said.

"All right. As you like. I can't say any more, can I?"

"No." He smiled at last, just. The medal caught the sun, and Beethoven scowled. Ruth wanted to have it, there and then, as if by holding it in her own hands safely she could make Pat's life perfectly secure to match.

"Can I come on Friday?"

"Yes. Of course."

She remembered the last concert, and the Professor saying the more nervous Pat was the better he played, and herself wanting just Pat alone, without the musical overtones.

"This nine months," she said, seeing Pat as the Professor saw him, "it won't be very good for you—musically, I mean . . ."

176

"No. It could finish anyone."

She was startled.

"It won't! Not after all you've achieved!"

"No, it won't," he said. "I've thought about it. I think about it all the time. They won't take that off me, not after all I've put in."

"What will you do? How can you, without a piano——?"

"Oh, there's some things obviously you can't do, but quite a lot you can. I'll have no excuse for not knowing the concerto for Backhaus, for example, with all that time to get it into my head. I shall take the music of everything I want in my repertory during the next few years and read it and read it and read it. And I'll keep my arms and my hands from rusting up, even if it means playing on the ruddy bedstead all night."

Ruth did not smile. His stubbornness did not surprise her, but the stark determination in his voice was daunting. It was useless—she saw it now quite clearly—to think that Pat existed apart from his music, because he didn't. She could not, any more, want him without it. She remembered the feeling that Pat's playing had created in her . . . Surely to be jealous of that part of him, and even of the Professor, was to deny what Pat actually was.

"Pat——"

The sun caught the medal and she thought Beethoven smiled.

"It will be all right," she said. "I know it will."

He put his hand on her shoulder.

"You think so?"

"It will be."

"You can make it all right," he said. "That's all there is to it. I can cope with the other."

"Yes. We've nothing to worry about."

"Not if you say so."

He smiled then, in the way that came so rarely. He took his arm away and undid the medal and put it around her own neck, doing it up under the warmth of her hair.

"It's like a ring," he said.

"But what about Friday?"

"He'll be there, just the same. He can watch me just as easily, can't he?"

"Yes," she said happily. "We won't let you go wrong."

Chapter Ten

✴

Sitting in the bus, waiting for it to go, she felt strangely happy. It was as if she was afloat on the sea of Rachmaninov again. She had a feeling that she was not on the seat at all, but drifting up against the ceiling, disintegrating like a dandelion clock, her mind scattered to the warm breeze. She tried to take a hold on herself, to stop smiling, aware of the suspicious glance of the Gas Board man on the seat opposite, but it was no good. She told herself that she was going to be very unhappy, but for this moment it had no meaning. The gold medal was warm on her breast, and Pat loved her.

The Gas Board man was blotted suddenly from her view by the totally unexpected figure of her mother, laden with shopping baskets. Ruth jumped.

Her mother said tartly, "I told you I was coming into Northend. You didn't hear me, any more than you've heard anything anybody's been saying for the last few days, but I did tell you. So don't look so surprised."

"No."

Ruth tried to gather the drifting seeds of her mind. She smiled at her mother.

"I saw you," her mother said tightly.

"Where?"

"Coming up the High Street about half an hour ago."

Ruth went on smiling, remembering the way Pat had smiled, and the hardness of his thigh against hers as they had walked up the street with their arms around each other. Her mother wasn't smiling.

"I take it he did have a shirt on when he appeared in court?" Her mother's voice was acid.

"Yes, of course. He wore his suit." He was wearing it again now, driving the Professor's Lotus back to London because the Professor had eaten too well and was sleepy. The Professor had said good-bye to her, as if he had meant it, but Ruth knew that he was far from being rid of her. She was sorry for him now. She almost loved him.

"What happened? Did he get off?"

"No. He's out on bail. He comes up again on the twenty-seventh."

"Oh, and then what?"

"He'll get nine months, they think."

Her mother's expression changed, the sharpness fading. She looked old, and sad, as she had when Ted and Barbara had started to go wrong.

"You wouldn't be told, would you?" she said. "You just didn't want to know, right from the start. The let-down wouldn't have been so hard if you'd taken it then. Now, well . . . I'm glad it's over."

"It isn't over."

"It will be when he's back in prison."

"No."

Ruth wasn't dandelion fluff any longer. She could feel the sap returning, the roots going down. Her mother did not reply. This was real, Ruth thought. Why had she thought she could just idiotically smile? She looked out of the window. The bus was leaving the bus station, heading for the sprawling amorphous belt of summer suburban concrete and prunus trees. Ruth did not feel she belonged anywhere.

Her mother said, "You've told him this? That you're going to—wait for him, I suppose is the phrase?"

"Yes."

"When are you going to see him again?"

"On Friday. He's playing in the Proms on Friday."

There was a long silence. Ruth was suspended again, the unhappiness balanced by fear of what her mother was going to say. Whatever, in fact, her mother was going to say would make no difference to what she had decided, but it could be nasty. She felt herself hardening, a core of resolution.

Then her mother said, "Would he find time, before the twenty-seventh, to come and have tea and meet your father?"

Ruth looked at her mother, astounded.

"*Why?*"

For one disbelieving moment she thought it was a Mrs. Cargill-Smith reason, because he was playing in the Proms, but she realized that her mother's reasons were far more profound. So profound that Ruth couldn't follow them.

"Why?" her mother repeated, as if she was hurt. "It's quite normal, Ruth. A quite normal invitation. Just to meet him."

"You—not to—not to warn him off?"

"Invitations to tea are generally issued with cordial intentions. This one is perfectly straightforward. Just to meet him."

"But I thought—I thought——"

"You thought I would forbid you to see him again? You were all geared up for a fight?"

"No. I wasn't thinking about it at all," Ruth said tightly. "Only about him."

"I'm tired of fighting," her mother said. "I've decided you're old enough to know what you're doing. If you want to go through with the difficulties and the hurt of the situation you've got yourself into, that's up to you. And I've decided I ought to know Pat a bit better before I pass judgement. When I heard him play on Saturday, God knows, I thought there must be more to him than the bit I've seen. That sort of thing must grow out of good intentions somewhere, whatever happens offstage."

"You won't—you won't nag him?"

"No. Look, I'm not condoning it. Don't think that. I want you to be happy, and I don't think he'll make you happy. But it's your choice. That's all there is to it."

"But it's the other way round too. That he should be happy."

"Yes. I agree. But don't be so naïve as to think you can make him so. He's his own worst enemy. You think that the love of a good woman is going to cure him—well, believe me, you won't be the first innocent girl to have this dream. I just want you to be realistic. If you want him, you must want him as he is now. Don't expect him to change. I'm not saying you can't help, but you can't change the nineteen years that happened before you met him. As long as you know this, Ruth. You understand what I'm saying?"

"Yes."

"I won't say this again."

Ruth looked at her mother and thought that she looked about sixty. "It will be all right," she said to her, as she had said to Pat. She knew it would.

"Yes, it might be. I just want you to know the other side though. And the nine months, remember. You——"

"Yes. Really. I've thought."

"It will be very hard."

"Yes. You won't say anything like this when he comes to tea?"

"No. Oh, no."

Her mother groped for her handkerchief and blew her nose. Ruth thought of Pat coming to tea, and her mother offering cake and Pat saying, "Thank you, Mrs. Hollis," like Gordon and Peter. Perhaps, if her parents were to take him without criticism, he might be glad of their friendship? Just a dull, modest home and perhaps Ted, even Peter, as a friend, and nobody to press and nag? It could give him a touch of the ordinariness that he so conspicuously lacked. It was an intriguing thought. Ruth was full of tenderness towards her mother. She was sorry for her.

She smiled at her and said, "Perhaps he could come on Saturday, after the concert's out of the way?"

"Yes." Her mother was fishing for something in her handbag. "Look. You might be interested. It was in the local paper."

She handed Ruth a cutting.

The cutting was headed, "Local pianist plays with Backhaus."

Ruth read, "To local musicians the most fascinating part of the evening came when the young Northend pianist, Patrick Pennington, took on the demanding part of soloist in the performance of Rachmaninov's Concerto No. 2 in C minor. Let it be said at once that this young artist has the technical equipment to go far indeed. Whether he will do so, pursuing the exacting part of truth and integrity in all that he attempts, or whether the aggressive element in his temperament will adversely affect the balance of his playing, remains to be seen.

"Given the evidence we were offered last night, the omens are good. There is beneath the brilliance of the attack a deep sensitivity. This was particularly evident in the thoughtful account of the slow movement which by its complete freedom from sentimentality was more deeply-moving than many a more extrovert performance aimed at the heart-strings. The case against, a tendency to lose this restraint in the more powerful bravura passages, resulted in an occasional harshness that was the only flaw in a very fine performance. Let us put this down to the exuberance of youth, and look forward to the further development of this very promising young player."

Ruth looked for the author's credit and found the initials E.C. She connected these with the grey-haired man who had been so moved backstage after the performance, whom she guessed was Pat's old teacher at school, but whether she was right she had no way of knowing.

She re-read the words, taking in the message. Whoever had written it, surely *knew* Pat? It fitted the situation perfectly. It was Pat.

"Here's another one," her mother said. "Out of *The Times*."

Ruth took it. It was very brief, from another initialled power. It set the scene in a few sentences and for Pat's part stated, "This was playing of extraordinary promise. If this boy can during the next few formative years control the many surging facets of this flowering talent, a player of exceptional stature should emerge."

This distant, uninvolved critic satisfied her even more. To both the critics Pat and the music were one, and what the newspapers were predicting about his musical future, so it would be with Pat himself. He might have declared that he had no regrets for what he had done but he had also revealed that, musically, he was preparing to get through the wilderness with the same thoroughness with which he had rehearsed his concerto. Given all that had happened, one could not hope for more.

She fingered the Beethoven medal, staring out of the window. Committed to the nine months herself, it occurred to her that she too might do a little homework, find out a little of what it was all about, even if merely enough to make herself useful in turning over. If Pat planned to commit a whole concerto to heart, she at least could learn when he had come to the bottom of a page. With Beethoven himself to encourage her . . . She smiled. She did not know why, primed with dire maternal pessimism, but the smile kept coming.

The Gas Board man, getting heavily to his feet, gave her a wink and said, "It's great to be young."

"Yes, God help us," said Mrs. Hollis, and put her handkerchief away.

And Pat, travelling down the fast lane of the clearway to London at seventy-five miles an hour, the Professor dozing in the passenger seat beside him, felt oddly optimistic, considering what lay before him. He started to whistle the Brahms waltz.

ABOUT THE AUTHOR

K. M. Peyton is the author of many distinguished books for young people, most recently *Flambards in Summer,* the third book in a historical trilogy, for which she received not only the Carnegie Medal but also the Guardian Award. Mrs. Peyton is an artist as well as an author, and often illustrates her own books. She and her husband, who is also an artist, live with their two children in Essex, England. Sailing, horseback riding, and music are activities shared by all the Peytons, and these interests are often reflected in Mrs. Peyton's novels.